the single dad's guide to recreation

a steamy, small town romantic comedy

welcome to climax
book one

Karen Grey

Published by HOME COOKED BOOKS
a division of Jasper Productions, LLC

Cover design © Flower Prince Designs

This is a work of fiction.

Names, characters and events are either a product of the author's imagination or are used fictitiously.

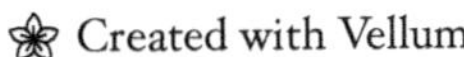 Created with Vellum

what readers are saying

"This author is truly a master at creating likable, three-dimensional characters." - *Laurie Reads Romance*

"Karen Grey has a lovely, deft touch with her characters, the plot, and with the world she's created." - *Bookbub review*

"Karen Grey has become an auto-buy author for me. I like her writing style/voice. She writes go-getter female characters and awesome male characters." - *Bookbub review*

"Full of humor, emotional depth and the perfect amount of spice." - *Bookbub review*

"The best blend of sweet and steam as well as angst and laughs." - *Bookbub review*

"So heartfelt and relatable - I was drawn in and hooked from the first page." - *Goodreads review*

"Made me laugh, tugged at my heartstrings, and threw in some steam for the triple crown win." - *Bookbub review*

"This romance has all the feels, it's romantic, and funny, and it's full of sizzling chemistry with wonderful characters you can't help loving." — *Bookbub review*

"Reading this is like immersing yourself in your favorite dramedy." - *Bookbub review*

content guidance

To the reader: my romance novels are all lighthearted and humorous and the main two characters are guaranteed to find a happy ending. However, they may run into a few obstacles along the way as well as need healing from incidents in their former lives. The list below is meant to give readers a generalized view of potentially triggering subjects within this novel.

- Use of expletives
- Sex/Nudity
- Alcohol use
- Death (described from past)
- Mental Health: (described from past)
- Reproductive health issues: (described from past)

If you'd like a more detailed list of content warnings (which may include spoilers) they are available at: karen grey.com/contentguidance

chapter
one

For most people, the answer to the question, "How do I get to Climax?" is personal. Intimate, even. But in our little Upstate New York town nestled between the banks of the Hudson and the rise of the Catskills, we have a ready answer: "No need to *get* to Climax, when you *live* in Climax."

No lie, it's our official slogan. I just passed a billboard with the words blazoned across it. The one that taunts me on my way to work every morning.

Which is why I came up with my version: "There's no getting to climax when you're a twenty-nine-year-old who lives with her parents. In Climax."

For the record, I did leave my hometown. After college, I moved to Atlanta for a great job in hotel management and set up house with my boyfriend. But when that life imploded, I came home to regroup. It was supposed to be a short stay, but my best friend Leia talked me into working for her at Climax Parks and Rec, managing children's programming. Then, just as I was thinking about leaving again, my parents' health went south. So, of course, I stayed on to help out.

Now I'm a little stuck.

But it's all good, as they say. My friends may needle me about playing Cinderella, taking care of everyone's needs but my own, but I think things have turned out fine. Better than fine.

Who needs a prince, anyway? I mean, those glass slippers look like a safety hazard, if you ask me. Don't even get me started on that ball gown. Shapewear hasn't been invented to cinch anyone's waist that tight. And it's not like I'm locked in my garret room. I chose to sleep under the sloping ceilings of the attic.

That Cinderella tag is just bull patties. I love being able to take care of my parents, I love being back in my hometown, and I love working with my best friends.

As I pull into the employees' parking lot at CPR—short for Climax Parks and Rec—the sun reflects off the glitter I'll never get out of my favorite cardigan. I'll admit that I could dial down the arts and crafts in the class I teach in addition to my admin work. My mother created the parent-toddler program we call Playgroup, and it's been the heart of CPR since before I was born. When she couldn't run it anymore, there was talk of canceling, but there was no way I was letting it die on my watch.

I'm not a parent; I've never been a parent. Due to the aforementioned life implosion, I'll likely never be a parent, so I'm not exactly qualified to teach anyone about parenting. But my mom assured me that the true purpose of the program is to, and I quote, "build community by giving new parents a space to connect with each other while their toddlers take part in age-appropriate activities."

I figured I could handle that.

I was already doing the work of one and a half people, since the adult programming admin left six months after I started and never got replaced. I figured I may as well make it an even two. I used my mom's notes and outlines, and I read tons of early childhood development books. I'm still sure that someone's going to walk in while we're singing "The Wheels on the Bus" and ask me what the halibut I think I'm doing, but it hasn't happened yet.

At the moment, however, I am questioning the wisdom of carrying the heavier-than-I-thought stack of boxes full of donated supplies from my car to the classroom instead of fetching a handcart first. But when you've got six kids under three showing up in twenty minutes, you don't have time for extra steps. So I tell my aching arms to shut the H-E-double-hockey-sticks up and use a hip to push open the heavy side door of the building that feels as much like a home to me as the house I grew up in. Successful navigation of the doorway accomplished, I just have to make it down the hall and somehow get the door to the playroom unlocked before my shaking biceps give out on me.

Note to self: get your well-padded hips and noodle arms to one of the fitness classes offered for free at your place of employment. I'm scrolling through the class schedule in my mind, wondering if I could squeeze in Jazzercise if I skipped lunch, when unfamiliar voices coming from the lobby catch my attention.

Peering between items sticking out of the top box, my stranger danger alert goes on high. The group of people in fancy suits aren't threatening in a *Hey kid, want to see my puppy in this white van* kind of way, but something about them feels off. They sure as sugar don't look like they're here to sign up for a softball team. Or participate in any other form of recreation. Plus, the center isn't even open yet, so how did they get in?

My grip slipping, I drag my focus back to getting the boxes down the hall. I can't help hearing their conversation as I pass, however. The soothing voice that first broke into my thoughts is interrupted by one with a foreign accent, something vaguely British. Or Swedish? Or some unidentifiable tiny European nation you'd find in a Hallmark movie?

Weirdly, *that* voice sounds familiar.

"You've got your work cut out for you here, Josh," he intones. "This place is a dump."

"It is a bit worn around the edges..." Soothing guy— must be Josh—tries to get a word in, but Euro Voice just talks over him.

"Can you believe this program schedule? I don't think our people are going to sign up for"—he pauses, and I swear I can hear him shudder—"Zumba or Quilting. We'll need a Pilates setup, of course. And CrossFit is a no-brainer."

"If the rest of the building is all chipped tile floors and drop ceilings like what's going on here," a judgy third person says. "You may as well raze this place to the ground and start over."

When I trip, probably on one of those chipped floor tiles, the words *raze this place to the ground* echo inside my head. Boxes fly out of my arms, art supplies roll in every direction, and I land with a thud. Wincing in frustration as well as pain, I crawl along the floor to clean up the mess, noticing for the first time that the tiles are stained as well as cracked.

"Miss, are you okay?"

When I catch sight of the face behind that soothing voice, I actually gasp. Talk about Prince Charming. Tall, check. Dark, check, the bronzed skin of his face framed by chocolate brown hair. Aaand handsome, check, with eyes as blue as the sky on a perfect summer day.

"Did you hit your head?" he asks, dropping to his knees next to me.

My mouth's probably flapping open and closed like a fish out of water, and the only words I'm coming up with are ones I cannot say out loud in my place of employment. Or even in my head. There are no kid-friendly substitutes for these words.

He holds out a hand. I take it. And just like in the movies, his touch sends a shiver through me. I swear romantic music swells.

Though that might be from the art room down the hall. Daisy does blast music when she's trying to get in the zone before class.

"Do you think you can stand?" he asks, his baby blues filled with concern. "Should I call nine-one-one?"

Blowing out a breath, I force my gaze away from the chiseled jaw mere inches from mine, from the full lips uttering the kindest words, and focus on the fabric of his trousers. "You're-you're going to ruin that suit."

"That's what dry cleaners are for," he says, his tone rougher than before. But in a good way. "I apologize, I should've offered to help with these boxes."

"It's my fault. I should've used a cart to move them

from my car." Easing my hand out of his, I scoot away so I don't crawl into his lap. "In fact, I think I'm going to get one right now. Avoid further disasters."

He looks uncertain, so I add, "I swear I'm fine. Just"—a silly high-pitched giggle rides the word—"ha-ha! Clumsy."

"If you're sure." Getting to his feet, he holds out his hand. Again.

I shouldn't touch him again, but I do. And there's that shudder, this time going straight to my core. Like somebody took a broom to the dust and cobwebs down there.

When he pulls me up, momentum drives me right into his chest, flattening my breasts against hard-as-granite pecs and knocking us both off balance. We do an awkward little dance to find our feet. Almost in slow motion, his eyes dip to my lips, and I lean in, needing his kiss more than I need my next breath.

"Josh?" Euro Voice echoes down the hall. "You're missing the thought shower."

I stumble back, muttering, "I'm going to get that cart now." And then I book it down the hall before I do anything else I'll regret.

By the time I return, the boxes are neatly stacked. The man that'll surely play a starring role in my dreams tonight even picked up the markers and glue sticks that flew out of the open crate I'd stupidly balanced on top.

I'm battling the urge to just grab him and kiss him when another man steps between us, flocked by the rest of the group. "You're needed up front, Josh. A/B testing will be required to maximize front-end user experience and..."

As his gibberish continues, the voice and face click,

and I realize why he sounded so familiar. "Elijah Ransom? Is that you?"

Pausing mid-monologue, he cocks his head to the side, like a bird. "It is. Do I know you?"

"Only since eighth grade." He continues to stare at me like I'm a particularly challenging puzzle, so I add, "When you moved to Climax?"

"My apologies, when I'm excited about a new project, my prosopagnosia escalates." Elijah presses his hands together in front of his chest and bows at me. "Remind me of your name?"

Josh places a light hand on my elbow, making my knees wobblier than a Jell-O salad at a Fourth of July picnic, and murmurs into my ear. "Prosopagnosia is commonly called face blindness. It's a neurological disorder that prevents people from recognizing even those they know well."

"Oh, well, I'm sorry for your loss," I say to Elijah. "I'm Avery Mills. It's nice to see you again, and nice to meet you, uh..."

As Josh lifts his hand from my arm and I catch the flash of gold on his ring finger, my words fade away. News flash: the man I've been drooling over for the past fifteen minutes is *wearing a wedding ring*. I may be a fudge up, but I don't mess around with married men.

Pasting on a polite smile, I step away from the group. "If you will excuse me, I need to get to work."

The word "work" seems to spark something in the suits, because they all begin to talk at once, vying for Elijah's attention. When I move to the cart, I can almost feel Josh wanting to follow, but he doesn't step up to help me. Before I can ogle him one last time, however, the director of Climax Parks and Rec steps into the foyer, and everyone stops talking again. Hands on hips, Leia Blake—aka my best friend/boss—lifts her chin to aim a glare at the man obviously in charge.

Aka, her on-again, off-again high school boyfriend, at least until he disappeared right before junior prom.

"What the fuck are you doing here, Elijah Ransom?"

chapter **two**

JOSH

Until today, I had no idea that big round eyes, a heart-shaped face, and perfect Cupid's bow lips were my catnip. In a cartoon, she'd likely have woodland creatures or elves flocking to her, but in real life, Avery Mills has cast a spell on me. When we touched, each and every part of me relaxed —except one, which she awakened from a deep, deep slumber—making me want to get as close to her as humanly possible.

Could be magic, could be a hallucination brought on by whatever industrial-strength cleaner they use on the floors, but whatever the cause, I cannot afford to be spellbound right now.

I cannot be thinking inappropriate thoughts while I'm working at my brand-new job. And not just any job, but one that I'm pretty damn sure was a pity hire. And not just at my brand-new pity hire job, but the job that involved moving my family to the middle of nowhere.

But I've only been in the Climax Parks and Rec center for fifteen minutes and it's clear that this part of my job is a disaster in the making. I'm hitting on women and making them drop things, and Eli is making enemies right and left.

When the new voice echoing through the foyer has my boss's face turning even paler than usual, I force my attention away from the magical Avery to the object of his dismay. Noting the venomous expression on the face of the petite brunette in the doorway, I step in before things go from bad to worse.

"Good morning, I'm Josh Harmon from Trede," I say, holding out my hand. "We're here to embed with your team. You know, assess the framework, perhaps do a minor re-org."

She ignores me. "Elijah Ransom, I said, why are you here?"

"As Josh explained, to interface." Eli bows at her, a gesture I've got to get him to stop using. Not only is it misplaced cultural appropriation, but people hate it. "Reduce the friction in the back end so we can optimize X-functionality."

Her mouth twists into an even deeper frown. "Did you forget how to speak English?"

One of the other team members places a hand on her shoulder. "It took me a while to understand them too. Basically, we're going to fix this place."

She stares at the hand until they remove it. "Who the hell said you could waltz in here and tell me what to do?"

Groaning inwardly at the obvious communication breakdown, I clear my throat. "Actually, the mayor. And the town council."

"For fuck's sake," she mutters.

An imposing, middle-aged woman sticks her head into

the doorway. "Center's opening in ten minutes, Leia. You'd best move this out of the foyer."

"Fine. Into my office, now." The woman called Leia steps out of the doorway and gestures down a hall behind her. As I pass, I hear her ask, "Can you handle the phones, Wanda?"

Wanda says something about needing to finish the Q2 books and tells Leia she has fifteen minutes.

As we all crowd into a tiny room stuffed to the gills with office equipment from the last century as well as bookshelves full of actual ring binders, I fully intend to stand closest to Leia, but my body has other ideas. It puts me right next to Avery. When the other Trede representatives squeeze in on her other side, I have to forcibly stop myself from touching her honey blond hair to find out if it's as soft as it looks.

It's official: my dry spell has gone on way too long. As I remind myself that there are two very good reasons why, things escalate further between Leia and Eli.

"Princess, you can't mean what you're saying," Eli is saying.

Leia's brown eyes practically shoot lasers at Eli. "I told you to never call me that again."

"Uh-oh," Avery breathes.

Leaning closer to her, I whisper, "Princess? Leia? As in *Star Wars*?"

She meets me halfway and whispers back. "Yep. It's his old nickname for her."

"First off, it's Leia," Leia snaps. "Or better yet, Ms. Blake."

"She's hated it ever since he left town," Avery whispers.

"Blake? But your last name is Butts," Eli says.

"Not anymore." Leia lifts her chin defensively. "Obviously, I didn't want my kids to have to endure the teasing I did in school, so I dropped it when I had the opportunity."

"You have kids?" Eli's squawks.

"Frankly, that's none of your business," Leia shoots back. "It is *my* business to run Climax Parks and Rec, so any changes to the building or programming need to be run by me."

Eli bows. Again. "Of course, of course. When we get to the front-end user flow—maybe even the A/B testing phase—your data sets will be invaluable. Perhaps we can even get you into a Mood Board meeting."

One of our team members begins to chant paint colors, and Leia looks like she's about to blow her top. I open my mouth to put a stop to it all, but before I can utter a word, Avery grabs my forearm, the sight of her plump bottom lip caught between her teeth rendering me speechless.

"You'd never know the two of them were an item in high school," she murmurs.

"Shit," I whisper. "Now everything makes sense."

With Avery so close, my hormone-muddled brain may be having a hard time focusing on the problem at hand, but I can still put two and two together. Or maybe one and one is more like it. I've wondered why Eli chose to move Trede to a small town in Upstate New York after founding the startup accelerator in California. Seems like this "Princess Leia" had something to do with it.

"Why don't you just build something new?" Leia asks. "Part of whatever fabulous building I hear you erected for... what's your business called? Treed? Like a dog with a raccoon?"

"It's spelled *T-R-E-D-E*," I say, like that's going to help.

"Trede is sourced from try," Eli explains. "To experiment, to strive. To have or gain knowledge of or by experience."

Leia rolls her eyes. "Of course you'd name your business a made-up word."

Without picking up on her scathing sarcasm, he nods. "We still haven't been able to get it into the dictionary, but we're working on it."

She waves a hand in his face like she's trying to erase him. "Whatever. My question is, why do you have to change *this* place? Why can't you just build a fancy gym or whatever for your employees?"

"Our campus has a world-class fitness center," he says. "Studies have shown that midday exercise increases productivity by three hundred percent."

"Great. I'll just see you and your flunkies to the door, and you can leave us alone."

"However," Eli continues, ignoring her shooing gesture. "In exchange for tax concessions, I have a mandate to give back to the town of Climax. So it seems obvious to begin with what I understand is its primary interface."

"Maybe we like our *interface* just fine the way things are."

"I'm afraid surveys say otherwise," I say, hoping to draw her ire away from Eli.

She narrows her eyes at me, and I get the distinct impression she hadn't really noticed me earlier. "Who are you and who gave you access to our survey results?"

"Josh Harmon, and the mayor's office," I answer as quickly as possible, hoping that a terse reply will counterpoint Eli's tendencies to overexplain.

"As Vice President of Community Engagement for Trede, it's Josh's job to dev-op," Eli says. "Run minification and caching, basically set up your sandbox for optimal flow."

"He just means that I'll be the point of contact as we digest consumer research and plug it into various models in order to create the best—*oof.*" The office door whacks me in the back, and I'm shoved right into Avery. When her eyes go wide, I throw my hands in the air. "I am so—"

"Whoops." A deep, mellow voice drowns out my apology, and the head and shoulders of a tall white man with a square jaw, deep-set brown eyes, and close-cut dark brown hair appear. "Sorry to interrupt, boss, but we've got a clog in the sink in the women's locker room again."

"I'd recognize that voice anywhere," Eli whispers, his head ticking back and forth between the Princess and the Hunk. "Blake. Leia Blake. As in Travis Blake. The handsome-but-brainless star football player at Climax High."

Still only halfway through the door, the man just shrugs. "That's me."

Thankfully, Leia leaves her office to deal with the plumbing issue, and I somehow get Eli and the rest of the Trede team out of the building and back to headquarters before anyone can do anything else to make my job harder. Back at the office, Eli gets sucked into meetings and I spend the rest of the afternoon giving myself a stern talking to regarding my priorities.

Namely, what's left of my family.

My two kids are at the top of the list. After everything

they've been through, they need stability. My parents follow. When I got the Trede job offer—for a position I'm pretty sure Eli made up out of thin air because he felt sorry for me—my parents put their travel-the-world retirement plans on hold and moved to Climax to help me out.

So I really need to stop drooling over a woman I need to interface with. Not suck face with.

Two days later, ramping up my energy as I approach CPR —the somewhat confusing way the locals refer to Climax Parks and Recreation—I turn on the charm that served me well in my career as a Wall Street fixer, even though I'm pretty sure that man doesn't exist anymore. The highs I used to get from being the guy who could always solve a problem just don't do it for me anymore.

Still, if I could put together a real estate LBO model at three in the morning when I really have no expertise in the field, I should be able to convince Princess Leia that her rec center is ripe for change. So I knock briskly on her door, and when she waves me in, I step inside with the smile I've been told is charming but confident. "Thanks for making time for me in your schedule, Ms. Blake."

"I didn't think I had a choice."

Arms crossed over her chest, chin lifted, she's already on the defensive. Obviously, I have lost ground to make up. "Listen, I truly am sorry about the ambush the other day. I had no idea that you were in the dark on the proposed changes."

"Elijah, or *Eli*, I guess"—her nose wrinkles like she can barely stand to say his name—"is to blame for it, I'm sure."

No skin off my nose to take the rap. "This was totally on me. It is my job to interfa—uh, liaise—between you, Trede, and the city government."

"Isn't Eli your boss?"

I shrug, keeping things easy. "He is. And I'm sure you know how that goes."

Her eyes narrow. "What do you mean?"

If I could shrink my six-foot-three body down to equal her five foot and change, I would. Instead, I sit across from her and hunch over, elbows on knees. "I can tell you two have a history. Which I'm sure makes this all... complicated."

She rolls her eyes. "You could say that again."

"Eli," I say on a chuckle, adding a *What can you do?* shrug. "When he's excited, especially when it's a new idea, he tunnel visions."

"So you've worked for him for a long time?" She picks up a pen and sits back in her chair to twirl it around her fingers.

"Actually, I just joined Trede a few months ago. But I've known him a long time. My, uh, wife—" It's still difficult to figure out how to refer to her, but I push on. "Worked on a startup with him their senior year in college. She vowed to never do it again."

She nods knowingly. "Because he's such a jerk?"

I shake my head. "Because she valued his friendship too much."

"So why are *you* working for him?" she asks, sitting forward.

This is an easy answer, even though working for the man is nowhere near easy. "He made me an offer I couldn't refuse. And it was a good fit for me and my family."

She taps the pen on her desk blotter and her gaze flicks to her computer monitor, a piece of equipment that looks like it's been there for twenty-five years. It seems like I've shifted things slightly, but I'm running out of time, so I go for broke. "Can I be frank, Ms. Blake?"

She puffs out a slightly less irritated sigh. "You can call me Leia."

"Leia, I honestly believe that if we work together—you and me and your staff—we can make this place the center of the community. Not just a community center."

Her eyes narrow again. "That sounds like an ad campaign."

"It just came out of my mouth, but we could use it." My hand goes to my heart. "It's not just words. I am a part of this community now. I want it to be a place where my kids can thrive."

That last line isn't bullshit, I remind myself. They're the reason I took the job in this tiny town. *That, and the fact that you couldn't get out of bed in the morning back in Manhattan.*

She sighs again, but this time it feels like surrender. "What would this 'working together' mean?"

"Well, I'd love to start with your survey results from the past few years."

She stiffens. "I hope you're not looking at numbers during COVID. Obviously—"

"Obviously, those have to be treated differently. But there are some useful dynamics at play."

"Like what?"

"Hey, Leia?"

At the sound of that sweet voice, my head whips around to lock in on its source.

"Did you hear back from the fire department about visiting—" Seeing me, Avery freezes. "I'm so sorry I didn't know you had a, uh... I'll just check in la—"

There's a ripping sound as she disappears and then reappears in the doorway before falling through it head-first, exclaiming, "Oh, sugar!"

Diving between her and the floor, I just manage to catch her shoulders and roll beneath her to cushion her fall. When she lands on top of me, every molecule of air whooshes out of my body, but I don't care. I could lie here forever with her draped over me like a plush, cozy, sexy blanket. For a few magical moments we just blink at each other. When she breaks the spell, scrambling to her feet muttering apologies and something about a ripped pocket, my nose follows her, my lungs shamelessly vacuuming up as much of her scent as I possibly can.

The door slamming behind her brings me back to earth. A pointed throat-clearing from Leia brings me back to my senses. "Are you okay, Mr. Harmon?"

Hopping to my feet, I hunch over, brushing off my trousers as I will my junk to calm down. "Oh, yeah. Fine. Now, where were we?"

Face hot, I reach for my briefcase and grab the reports I brought along. Eighty-five percent sure she's a gal who likes a graph, I pull a stack of colorfully printed pages from my briefcase. Still needing a moment, I tip my head toward a table and chairs by the window. "Mind if I lay these out over there?"

"Sure. Whatever."

I turn my back as I spread out the bait and release a tiny breath of relief when she appears at my side. When she picks up a spreadsheet, I shift into full-on wonk-mode.

Five minutes later I've got her wrapped in demographics and percentages, all adding up to what she must see is truly incontrovertible data.

"Essentially, you're serving less than twenty percent of the citizens in Climax. Don't you want to expand that?"

She flicks a hand at the higher end of the income scale on one graph. "The eastside people have their golf clubs—"

I counter with a tap at the other end, the so-called wrong side of the tracks. "It's not just the high end of the earning spectrum. It's the low end too. You'd like to build diversity, right?"

She straightens, chin jutting out, arms crossing again. "We always have."

"But you can do better?"

Her attention goes back to the reports, and she picks up the programming proposal to flip through it. "So you're talking about adding programs? Where am I going to get the budget for that?"

"Trede has allocated resources to support any changes for a year—including building upgrades—but in order for the city to commit to adding line items to its permanent budget, we have a mandate from the mayor's office. All programming must be at eighty percent capacity by the end of the next fiscal year. Which means we should do our best to make changes to the schedule by September."

She fumbles her pen. "But that's just a couple months away. What happens if we don't?"

"In order to make the changes permanent, you'll have to consider cuts." I tap the graphs with enrollment data. "And the mayor agrees that the Climax population could be better served."

Tapping a line on the proposal, she makes a noise in the back of her throat. "Avery's toddler class is on this list. We can't lose Playgroup."

"Well, uh..." Just the mention of the name Avery has me skipping off to hearts-and-rainbows land, and I fumble as I search for the chart illustrating childcare statistics in the area. "Right. So, as you can see, the county is in dire need of more daycare, while the parent-toddler program enrollment has been falling for years."

"But it's magical," she says, her voice infused with a different emotion than she's used before. Something I can't quite identify, but it probably has to do with the bewitching Avery. "And it's a community builder. Kids from Playgroup participate in sports when they get older. Their parents take classes."

Not just because participation would mean spending time with the program's teacher, I say, "It sounds like something I'd love, honestly."

Leia's smirk is dismissive. "You're a little old."

"I'm not kidding," I say quickly, hand to heart. "I mean with my son. He's just about to turn two. And we don't know many other families in town yet."

"Well, there is room in the class..."

I have to bite my tongue to avoid pointing out the reason: enrollment is low.

"Hmm. You should try it." She raises her chin as she considers me. "You might find out that you don't want to cut it."

"How about this?" I say on a clap, like we've just agreed on everything. "I commit to taking the class and you'll take a serious look at other ways to utilize the space and staff so we can best serve that age group. The children *and* the parents."

Her sigh is heavy, but it's less dismissive, more *You've made your point*. "Fine. As long as I don't have to deal with Mr. Ransom."

Time to close, Harmon. "I will be your primary contact. He does have an entire company to run, after all."

"Maybe you could remind him of that, so he'll stay away?"

With her brows raised and lips pursed, I'm pretty sure I've got my deal and her number. "I'm on it."

Her eyes scan the reports. "Can I keep these?"

"Of course." I pick up my bag and then add, "With your permission, I'd like to meet with other team leaders. Just to get their insights."

She snorts as she picks up my proposal and crosses back to her desk. "Good luck with that. Especially with Carl Conrad. His bark is worse than his bite, but he does bite. Our office manager, Wanda, has tons of institutional knowledge but don't bother her until you know exactly what you need, or she'll give you nothing."

She pauses, tapping her pen on the desk. "Daisy, who directs our art program, is kooky but she knows her stuff. Avery runs all children's activities, but she'll be angry to hear that you're thinking about cutting Playgroup. Her swear words may be cutesy, but she's tougher than you'd think." She pauses, and I wonder how many more warnings she has to hand out about her staff. "My recommendation? Start with Travis."

"Travis? The ex-football player?" Also known as the third point of an old love triangle between Leia and my boss?

She nods definitively. "He knows everyone in town. He'll be a good resource."

On my way out the door, I'm almost giddy at the prospect of seeing Avery again. But as I review the last few minutes of our conversation, I have to wonder if I just got played.

chapter
three

In what I'm now referring to as the Before Josh Times, I slept like the dead at the end of every day. But in the After Josh times, I wake in the middle of each night all... hot and bothered. Which is not only embarrassing, it's wrong. I lie there, hands pressed to the mattress to keep them away from my private parts, reminding myself that the man I'm lusting over—the man I literally *fell on top of*— is married. I'm not sure what it'll take for my subconscious to get the message but avoiding him seems like the best tactic.

It would be easier if he'd stop calling me.

I love being busy, but the new stressors added to my very full schedule mean that everything takes a bit more out of me. Frankly, I usually get a little high from ticking off the many items on my many to-do lists. But this week, my sleep has been compromised, which means that everything else suffers.

I'm lecturing myself on the importance of good sleep

hygiene as I push a cart loaded with supplies to the canasta club meeting. When I pass the open door of the art room, catching sight of the man of my dreams in a passionate discussion with Daisy, CPR's art teacher, I crash the dang cart right into the wall. "Son of a nutcracker!"

"Are you okay, Avery?" Daisy calls.

"I'm fine," I yell back. "It's just the, um, fudged-up wheel on this thing."

I'm crouched on the floor playing fifty-two pickup times ten with the canasta cards when I get a whiff of the scent that makes a beeline directly from my nostrils to my Virginia.

"Here, let me help." His fancy leather shoes squeak, and when Josh squats next to me, I've got a front-row seat for a pair of masculine, muscled thighs straining to be contained by khakis. I have a long-standing policy to avoid sex with men whose thighs are smaller than mine, and Josh definitely passes that test. Not that I should be keeping score.

"I've got it," I protest, even though I've stopped cleaning up to watch his large, capable hands collect the playing cards.

"Avery?"

He's looking at me like he just asked a question which I obviously missed because I was fantasizing about other things those hands might do. Thankfully, when he holds out a stack of cards, I catch sight of that dang wedding ring. "No. I can't. But thank you."

Taking the cards and dropping them onto the cart, I hustle away to drop the supplies off before I do anything else I'll regret. Fifteen minutes later, when I pass the art room again on my way back to the office and Daisy yells my name, I'm surprised by the sharp tone in her voice.

I mean, what's she got to be mad about? She was the one making googly eyes at Josh while they talked about... whatever they were talking about.

When I pause in the doorway, she grabs me by the elbow, pulls me inside, and shuts the door behind me. "Avery Mills, what were you thinking?"

"Uh... when?"

"When you said you couldn't meet with Mr. Harmon!"

"Meet with Mr. Harmon? What are you talking about?"

"What are *you* talking about?"

"Whatever you and he were talking about."

"What did you think he was talking about?"

"I... uh, thought he was hitting on me."

"Hitting on you?"

Right. It would be ridiculous that someone like him would flirt with someone like me when whimsical, winsome, willowy art teachers are hanging on his every word. Even if he wasn't married.

"You have to talk to him." Daisy gets right in my face like I've been staring off into space. Like I probably was.

"Why?" I ask, a little too defensively.

"He's meeting with all the team leaders."

I am so confused right now. "Leaders of what?"

"CPR? The place where you work?"

"You mean the department heads?" Suddenly exhausted, I drop into a chair and trace a finger along the table etched with the ghosts of art projects past. "I don't get it."

She sits kitty-corner to me. "This is our chance to

communicate our priorities while they're still in the design phase."

"They who? And what design phase?"

"Trede is planning major upgrades at CPR." She hops up to grab a folder from her desk. After slapping it down in front of me, she claps her hands with a little squeal. "The new place is going to be awesome."

"But"—I look around the room as her words begin to sink in—"what about the old place?"

"Oh yeah. I'll be *so sad* to say goodbye to these dropped ceilings with stained and broken tiles." She rolls her eyes so hard it looks painful. "And the busted, out-of-date equipment that never gets replaced." She flicks a graceful hand in the direction of some old machine that hasn't worked in so long I'm not even sure what it was used for. "Not to mention the mysterious stink in the kitchen." She shudders briefly before wagging a finger back and forth in time with her words. "This complex was hastily built in the nineteen seventies and poorly maintained since, and you know it."

"Yeah, but..." I squirm in my chair, trying to find a defense for our poor old rec center.

"And look at all the things they want to add!" Daisy opens the folder and jabs a finger at a colorful printout. "Look at this mockup for the art room. All that natural light! I could finally teach pottery."

"You already teach pottery." Since I manage the programs, I know this is the case.

"For beginners. With only one working wheel and no kiln, all they can do is pinch pots." She jumps up from her chair and spins in a circle, her skirt swooping around her legs in a perfect swirl. "Just think! We could be excited about coming to work instead of worried that the ceiling will leak or the toilet will be clogged."

I have to stifle a groan because... she's right. I guess I need to talk to Josh. I just hope I can do it without rubbing up against him like a cat in heat.

chapter
four

JOSH

My mom got a little too excited when I announced that I'd be taking Percy to Playgroup a couple mornings a week going forward, which has me worried that running around after an almost-two-year-old is harder than they'd expected. My parents volunteered to take over as primary caregivers so I could go back to work, but I know all too well that summer days taking care of kids can be long ones. They are young grandparents, and in great shape, but I'll be the first to admit that my kids are a lot.

I'm also a little worried that I won't be able to get through the class without embarrassing myself. That my attraction to this program's leader will be all too obvious. So, for the entire drive from our house to the Parks and Rec center, I give both me and my son a pep talk.

"I bet it'll be fun to play with other kids your age, Percy."

As he whacks the back of the seat with a stuffie, Percy shouts, "Pay!"

Good reminder, Josh. You'll pay in more ways than one

if you screw up this job just because you can't keep your lust in check.

The toy goes flying into the front seat just as I pull into a parking spot. Before he can let out a howl of disappointment, I ask, "Ready to play with new toys?"

I learned pretty early on that one of the secrets to living with little kids is distraction followed by redirection. He's still chanting something that sounds vaguely like "new toy" as I unbuckle his car seat. Since we're running late, I scoop him into my arms. "Run?"

"Wun!"

I located the Playgroup classroom after my meeting with Leia—not that I was hoping to run into Avery, just making sure I knew where to go—and I sprint down the hall toward it now, with Percy giggling in my arms. The door is closing as we approach, so I call out, "Wait, please!"

Instead of opening the door wider, the woman of my dreams steps into the hall. When she sees me, she closes it firmly behind her, giving me a look like, *What do* you *want?*

"I'm here for the class," I say, a little breathless.

"Cass!" Percy shouts.

She flinches, like she hadn't noticed the toddler on my hip, but then her narrowed gaze zeroes back in on me. "What? Did you rent a kid so you could spy on me?"

"I, uh—" I falter, wondering if she really thinks I'd rent a kid. "I'm not here for work. I'm here to take part in the class. This is my son."

An entire movie's worth of emotion plays across her face as her eyes shift between my little guy and me, but I'm not sure if it's a rom-com or a disaster film.

"I suppose you do look alike." Her tone and expression

remain stiff until she turns to my son, and then it's all sunshine and rainbows. "What's your name, friend?"

"Pussy."

She blinks slowly. "Your name is... Pussy?"

"It's *Percy*." I clear my throat. "He's still, uh, working on his *R*'s."

She swallows a laugh, but I don't manage to squelch mine.

Avery crouches until she's nose to nose with my son. "Are you named after Percy Jackson?"

As Percy nods vigorously, I shake my head no. "It's a family name on his mom's side."

Before I can explain our family situation, the door behind her opens suddenly and a panicked woman whispers, "Avery, we've got a blowout."

Avery grimaces. "Let me guess. Theo?"

When the woman nods, Avery just turns up the wattage on her smile. "Good thing the weather's nice."

Moments later, everyone but Avery, Theo, and Theo's caregiver has moved outside so that a poopy mess can be cleaned up in the playroom. As the toddlers run around the small, fenced-in yard, the other parents introduce themselves to me.

"You play tennis?" Another dad in the group, a broad-shouldered guy with a close-cut Afro, holds out his hand. "Paul Coleman. We're always looking for players in the league."

"I do, but probably not as well as you," I say, trying not to wince while his hand crushes mine. "You've got quite a grip there."

"Yeah, sorry about that. Give me your number." He looks up from his phone. "Unless you play pickleball."

I have a feeling there's a right and wrong answer here, but I just give him the truth and hope for the best. "Uh, no. I don't."

He brushes an exaggerated *Whew* across his brow. "I'll get you on the roster."

"That'd be great. I'm new to the area and don't know many people. I have to work around my kids' schedules, but if you're okay with that…"

"I got you. My wife's the one with the big salary too."

"I'm a widower," I explain. "So it's just me."

"Oh my goodness," one of the moms says, appearing next to me. "I'm so sorry for your loss."

"Thanks. It's been tough, but we're getting through it. My parents have been a big help."

"It's good you have their support." Another mom steps up, tipping her chin at Percy. "Is he your only child?"

"I have a little girl too. She'll be in first grade in the fall."

I'm saved from further interrogation by a squabble on the climbing structure. By the time that's settled, Avery has returned.

"Theo and his granddad went home to clean up," she says. "It's still a bit fragrant inside, so I think we'll stay out here."

The children flock around Avery like cartoon birds and mice around Cinderella. At her instruction, they plop down crisscross applesauce, and she does an admirable job of getting them to sit without squirming too much, or, as in the case of Percy, sitting too close to his neighbors. I follow the parents to a couple of picnic benches nearby.

"I'm so happy to see you all today!" Avery says, her expression as cheery as her tone. "I'm happy to see Liam and Amelia and Olivia and Samar and Naomi. And the newest member of Playgroup, Percy."

She sweeps her gaze over all of the kids as she says, "Can everyone say hello to welcome Percy?"

A chorus of *Hello, Pussys* has me wondering if we should start calling Percy by his middle name.

Avery claps her hands together. "First, we'll read three stories. Then we'll have building time before snack. After that, we'll learn a new game. Then we'll have more free play before it's time to go home."

After catching nods and "okays" from only two children and one adult, she adds, "Can I see hands for everyone who heard the plan?"

It takes a bit of prodding but once everyone either raises a hand or gives her a verbal confirmation, Avery whips a stack of books out of a bag behind her little chair.

She doesn't use puppets or a felt board. All she seems to need is a musical voice and expert storytelling skills to keep them enthralled through three entire picture books. I don't think I've ever seen Percy sit still for so long without being constrained by a high chair or booster seat. And I'd be lying if I said I wasn't fully entranced too.

After the stories, Paul and another dad haul a box of cardboard bricks outside and Avery suggests that we all join in the fun. Some child-parent pairs work together easily, and some require gentle coaching from Avery to avoid a power struggle or a tantrum. I'm not surprised when Percy is more excited about knocking a tower down than building it. I'm even a bit proud that, instead of getting frustrated, I turn it into a game. By the fifth tower, Percy and a little girl count along with me as I stack the blocks before they kick them over.

Just as I'm running out of silly things to do with the blocks, like attempts at juggling or wearing one as a hat, Avery brings out a tray with cups of juice and little bowls of graham crackers. She checks to make sure Percy doesn't have any food allergies before getting the kids settled at a child-sized picnic table.

While the kids snack and the adults socialize, I find myself wondering if doing more parent-child activities would've made Lisa's postpartum depression easier to manage. Or if I'd been home more instead of practically living at the office, we could have participated together. Before I can get too maudlin, the hour and fifteen minutes is up, and Avery's waving goodbye to the class at the gate.

So far, it seems that Avery's level of expertise is exceptional. Much higher than what you'd expect from looking at her resume. Unfortunately, the cost of running this playgroup is so high, it'll take some doing to justify keeping it.

I do hope this won't be its last summer.

And if it has to be cut, I really hope it won't be me who has to drop the axe.

chapter
five

AVERY

Despite his claim that he's in over his head, Josh is a natural with his little boy. He had me in stitches when he pretended to eat Percy's crackers, going on and on in a terrible French accent about how they were "magnifique." In my book, a buttoned-up man being silly with a kid is hotter than a shirtless firefighter in a calendar photo shoot.

Meanwhile, I've tried to schedule a meeting with Josh, but something or another has needed my attention at the end of each Playgroup meeting. Then, once I get back to my office, ten things or another demand my intervention, and I never get around to calling him.

Adding to the drama around CPR, Leia cannot stop complaining about how Elijah keeps showing up with his entourage to take photos and measurements and notes. She claims her grouchiness is all about the threats to the center, but I'm pretty sure whatever happened between her and Eli before he left town is upsetting her too. I guess even best friends keep some secrets from each other.

I know I have.

As I approach the atrium where my boss-friend and I share lunch at least a couple times a week, all her attention is on the contents of a manila file folder.

"Best tacos in town coming right up!" I say as I set the tray on the picnic table.

Flinching, she closes the folder and shoves it in her tote bag. "Great! Let's eat!"

There's something off about her chipper tone. Mostly that it's chipper. "Are you hiding something from me? Like whatever's in that file?"

"Pfft." She waves my accusation away. "I just don't want those reports to get grease-stained. What'd you get?"

I let it go for the time being because I'm too hungry to argue. "I didn't eat breakfast so I may have gone overboard. You have a choice of bean, chicken, barbacoa, or tofu."

"I'll take the chicken and barbacoa, if that's okay." She unwraps a to-go spork and pulls out the containers of sides. "Not in the mood for vegetables."

We're both quiet as we divvy up the food and dig in, but after she takes a long sip of her soda, Leia grumbles, "Why do the assholes all have to be so good-looking?"

"Tell me about it," I say with my mouth full. "That describes every person in your office the other day."

She shakes her head. "Travis is a good guy. He's just, you know, the engine's running but nobody's driving."

"Come on now. Travis may not have a college degree, but he's got people smarts."

"True. You thought the others were hot?"

Her tone is way too casual as she picks up a plastic cup

of salsa and drags a chip through it, but two can play this game.

"I mean, Elijah filled out nicely," I say. When she stuffs a giant scoop of chip and guac into her mouth, my suspicions are confirmed. Leia is fastidious about taking small bites and chewing thoroughly, unless she's upset about something. "Are you still hung up on him?"

"Of course not," she argues with her mouth full. Also something she never does. "What about the other guy?"

"Which one?"

"The one who signed up with his kid for Playgroup. What was his name?"

Her tone is so fake, I know she knows his name, but I also know she's not going to let this go, so I just give her what she wants. "Josh. His name is Josh."

"Riiight. You think he's cute."

"Well, he is. Objectively." Feeling my cheeks heat, I do my best to shrug it off. "He's also married, Leia."

"Really? I didn't get that vibe from him."

"Anyway, I'm not interested." A ping on my phone gives me an excuse to change topics. "That reminds me, I need to get one of your kids to help me with this thing."

"What's wrong with it?"

"You don't know how lucky you are that you married and divorced Travis before apps. Peter and I shared all of them—TV streaming, music, you name it. And now, I can't get his stupid preferences to stop screwing up my algorithms. I never liked heavy metal, but now?" I shudder. "I can't stand it. Every time it shows up in my feed, I can't press the thumbs down fast enough."

"Why do you want my kids' help?"

"Don't teenagers know everything about this stuff?"

Leia freezes, spork midair. "I sure hope not. Travis and I share all our accounts for that very reason. So we can try and stay ahead of them."

"Good luck with that." I snort. "Oh, hey, that reminds me. I've had some parents in the toddler group ask about babysitting. Do you think the twins would be interested?"

"Probably not. Whenever I ask them about it, they say they're too busy." Leia throws a chip at me. "And don't think you're going to get away with changing the subject that easy."

"I don't know what you mean." I take a big bite of taco like I couldn't care less about the first guy in I don't know how long to make me feel all fluttery inside.

Before I can shove another bite in, she reaches across to grab my wrist. "I want my best friend to be happy, that's all."

"Did you not hear what I said? First off, Josh is married, so it doesn't matter if I find him attractive."

"Are you sure?" She frowns. "I feel like he was checking you out the other day."

"He's wearing a wedding ring."

She stares off to the left like she's trying to picture it. "I didn't notice. And what's the second thing?"

"Even if he were available, I've got too much going on right now. And too much baggage," I add before shoving another bite in my mouth.

She slaps her hands on the table. "Just because Peter skipped out on you does not mean every man is going to do the same."

Even though I brought up his name first, I can't let her go further down this road. What really happened between Peter and me will never see the light of day. "Says the woman who hasn't been on a date in... how long has it been?"

"Trying to keep track of two teenagers while running this place—" She gestures vaguely at the building surrounding us. "I'm way too busy to date."

"Pot calling the kettle bla-ack," I intone.

"Who's dating who?" a deep voice asks from behind me.

I snort and Leia rolls her eyes. "We have no gossip for you, Travis."

Leia's ex and the center's athletic director sits sideways on the picnic bench and leans over the remains of our lunch. "Oooh, is this from Tito's?"

When he reaches for it, Leia grabs the paper tray and holds it out of reach. "Tacos for tea."

You'd never think that a lifelong jock would be as into town gossip as he is sports ball rules, but Travis is the first to know anything in this town. He claims it's for the welfare of all the kids he's in charge of. I think it's because he was a yenta in another life.

He rubs his hands together with glee, but I tune out as soon as I realize that he's talking about their teenagers' friends. Travis and Leia do a remarkable job of co-parenting post-divorce, but I don't need to hear about teen love lives. Not when mine is nonexistent.

"Oh, and the person from Trede who was with Eli the other day?" Travis says after eating the last bite of Leia's chicken taco.

My ears prick up at the topic change, but I keep my eyes on my phone.

"Josh?" Leia asks.

"I didn't get his name. The tall, short-haired one."

"Josh. Josh Harmon." Clearly, Leia's saying his name loudly to get my attention, but I continue to pretend I'm engrossed in emails.

"Got it." Travis taps his temple like he's filing away the intel. The man may not know a single Washington politician or state capital, but he knows the full name of every child in this town and most of the adults as well. "Anyhoo, I saw him chatting with Daisy outside the coffee shop this morning and they looked pret-ty cozy."

The green-eyed monster stirs low in my belly. CPR's art teacher is everything I'm not. She's willowy; I'm pear-shaped. She's a vibrant redhead; I'm a washed-out blonde. She's talented; I'm just a paper pusher.

"Pfft," Leia says. "That's a work thing."

"How do you know?" I ask before I can stop myself. I mean, they did the re-org meeting last week. Now they're having coffee? Why is this information making me so angry?

Leia's brows go up like *I see you*, but she just says, "He's meeting with all CPR"—she pauses to make air quotes—"team leaders."

"Daisy doesn't coach a team," Travis says, looking genuinely confused.

I pat him on the forearm. "She means department heads."

"Ohhh." Travis scratches his chin. "I should probably return his calls then, huh?"

"Yes, you should." Leia says. "And then report back to me afterward."

"I'll do it now, chief." With a salute, he stuffs the last bite of her barbacoa taco in his mouth and jogs to the door leading to the gym and his office.

Leia sighs. "You know what? Maybe it's better if you avoid that guy. I can talk to him for you."

"Josh?"

She just nods, balling up taco wrappers and stuffing them into the bag, but her gaze darts to her tote bag.

"But I'm a team leader. I should meet with him," I argue, even though I've been spending the past week avoiding it. Suddenly, the hair on the back of my neck goes up as I remember the look on her face after she stowed those file folders. "You *were* hiding something from me when I walked up."

"No, I wasn't."

"Yes, you were."

"Wasn't."

"Let me see those files, then."

I reach for her bag, but she moves it off the table. "Can't. Confidential stuff."

"I call bullnickles."

She meets my gaze and holds it for several seconds before dropping her bag on the bench and her head in her hands. "I guess you'll find out soon enough."

Wishing I could rewind the past few minutes—heck, the entire past week—I force the question past my suddenly rigid jaw. "Find out what?"

She sighs heavily.

"What is it, Leia?"

She winces, swallows, and then blurts, "Playgroup's on the chopping block."

chapter
six

JOSH

Despite every effort to juggle my work and home lives, my week somehow goes from bad to worse. On pretty much every front and according to every metric, nothing is going my way.

At Climax Parks and Rec, except for a short meeting followed by a brief chat with the art teacher when I happened to meet her in line at Happy Endings bookstore and coffee shop, I haven't been able to pin down a single team leader. On top of that, Eli keeps inventing reasons to visit the center, so Leia is furious with me.

Worse, my daughter Mabel has been super unhappy at the day camp I found for her, hoping to give my parents a break. According to my mom, Mabel goes directly from the car to her room at the end of every day and won't tell any of us what she's upset about. I've left messages for the camp director, but they haven't returned my calls.

The only bright spot has been Playgroup. It's such a great program, I've started to look into ways to keep it around. It may serve a small population, but every caregiver and child in the group seems to benefit from it. Percy clearly loves the opportunity to play with kids his age and has fallen head over heels for Avery.

Almost as hard as I have. From her toddler-taming abilities to her sunny approach to each and every problem, I just want to bask in her warmth every second of the day.

But that way lies madness. Or at least a broken heart or three.

With my track record, the possibility that things would go well are zero to none. So I can't risk even asking her on a date—because when I screw up, which I inevitably will— my kids will be hurt all over again.

With all this circling the drain in my brain, I do my best to focus on my job, since I finally have an appointment scheduled with another CPR lead this morning. Carl Conrad is the man Leia warned me the most about, but he's the only person I've been able to pin down.

When I arrive at the center for our meeting, I take the long way around the building so I can avoid the Playgroup room, repeating the mantra *Stay away from Avery* the entire way. But when I knock on the Facilities Manager's office door, I hear Avery's laughter on the other side.

Shit.

"Come in," a gruff male voice calls.

As I reach for the door, it swings open. Thrown off balance, I stumble forward. When I grasp Avery by the upper arms to keep us both from falling, a memory of a dream I had early this morning flashes through my mind. One so filthy, even a microsecond of replay has my hips moving toward her like I'm packing a heat seeking missile.

"Oh, it's you," she says in a strangled tone that makes

me wonder if she can tell what's going on behind my zipper.

"You who?" the gruff voice barks.

"I-I'm sorry," I stammer, releasing my grip on her and pressing into the doorframe to let her pass.

"You-you're fine," she stammers back before escaping past me.

I grip the door handle hard, only allowing myself three seconds to watch her swaying hips as she walks away, but even that has me in need of a cold shower. When I face the man I'm supposed to be meeting, however, the disapproving look on his face does the trick.

Leaning across his desk, Carl Conrad asks, "What are your intentions with Miss Avery?"

"I'm-uh, my... intentions?"

He stands, and it's like Paul Bunyan rising before me. When Leia had described the facilities manager, I'd pictured an older man. But this guy is not only young, he's jacked. Despite his grumpy expression, I'm sure the ladies find the piercing forest green eyes and shoulders barely contained by his uniform shirt to be insanely attractive.

"You'd better not be thinking of messing around with her."

"I would never, um, mess around with her." There's no way I'd win if it came to a battle with this guy, so I guess it's better to know now. "Are you two... together?"

"No," he scowls, all *How could you even say that?* "She's like a sister to me. And she's been hurt. I don't want to see her hurt again. You get me?"

Each phrase he growls out is punctuated by a jab of his finger in my direction, so my hands fly up in the air in defense. "I got you. I have no plans to mess around with

Avery. She's my kid's teacher." When he narrows his eyes, I add, "In the playgroup."

He grunts like he doesn't believe me. I decide it's best to pivot, even though it looks like I've already lost the support of the one person Leia told me I really had to win over. "So, as you've likely gathered, I'm Josh Harmon from Trede. Thanks so much for making time to meet with me."

He crosses his arms, tucking his hands in his pits, which makes his biceps bulge. "Not like I had a choice."

Common refrain around here. "Still, I appreciate it."

"And what is this meeting for exactly?"

"I'm here to listen."

"To what?"

I don't have to shrink my body in order to cede status to this giant, but I do need to make him feel valued. "Your ideas. Your concerns. Anything you want to tell me about CPR. We at Trede have resources put aside for improvements, from programming to the facility, and since you're in charge of the facility..." I trail off and sweep a hand around his cramped office.

"Hmmph." He drops into his chair. "You really want to hear what I've got to say?"

He hasn't invited me, but I take the seat opposite him anyway. "Leia says you know more about what this place needs than anybody."

He narrows his eyes at me. "How long you got?"

I pull out my tablet and stylus and prepare to take notes, giving myself a teeny-tiny mental high five. "As long as it takes."

By the end of the week, both Mabel and I could really use some fun, so when I hear a coworker raving about their experience strawberry picking at a place called Bedd Fellows Farm, I decide to take the kids. When my mom begs off Saturday morning, saying that she and my dad have made a pickleball date, I push away the worry that I won't be able to handle the kids on my own.

Mabel likes to know the plan ahead of any new experience, so I do a bit of research. As I study the farm's basic website, I wonder if I know the Bedd family. My freshman year roommate's last name was Bedd, and he grew up on a farm.

Sam and I only lived together one year. He went home most weekends, and I rushed a fraternity, so we didn't socialize much, but I always liked the guy. Thinking it would be nice to reconnect, I'm actually hoping I get to see him. Once we arrive, however, the kids and I get caught up in the activities. The kids pet the adorable calf and taste the strawberry milk, and we buy a jar of local honey for my mom. I'm admiring a hand-knitted sweater, picturing it hugging Avery's curves, when Mabel asks, "Where are the strawberries, Daddy?"

Looking around the barn, I notice a sign over a door and point to it. "Can you read that?"

"Strawberry picking this way," she reads, loudly and without hesitation, before making a beeline for the door. It takes me a moment to scoop up Percy, so by the time I find her, she's chatting with a redhead standing behind a table piled with buckets.

"You pay for the bucket, Daddy," Mabel explains. "If you save it and use it again next time, you pay less."

She frowns, turning back to the woman behind the

table. "But why do we have to pay for the bucket if we already have it?"

The woman seems a little stumped by Mabel's logic, so I jump in. "We're really paying for the strawberries, sweetie. They're incentivizing returning to pick again and avoiding waste by giving us a discount the next time."

"Ohhh," Mabel says.

"Exactly," the woman says before turning a relieved smile my way. "I'm Molly, by the way."

After I introduce myself and Percy, we decide to pay for one large bucket. As Molly swipes my card, a man steps up to say something quietly in her ear. A blush reddens her pale skin from chest to hairline, and she swats at him playfully. When he straightens, a taller, broader version of my old roommate grins at me.

"This might sound weird," I ask, "but... do you happen to have a brother named Sam who went to Cornell?"

"Sure do." The man hooks a thumb over his shoulder. "If you take the pony cart to the upper fields, he's driving."

Mabel gasps. "I wanna go on the pony cart!"

I shrug. "I guess that's what we're doing, then."

The couple shows us where to wait, but when the cart comes down the lane, Mabel's eyes grow wide. "That's a big pony."

"Pretty sure that's a full-on horse." I squeeze her shoulder. "You still want to ride?"

When she nods vigorously, I turn my gaze back to the incoming cart. The man driving is backlit, so I shade my eyes with my free palm. "Sam Bedd? Is that you?"

The driver tips his head to the side, and he pulls on the reins to stop the horse. "Josh Harmon? What the fuuu—" He clears his throat, obviously noticing the kids at my side. "What the fork are you doing here? I thought you lived in the city."

Before I can explain, Mabel looks him right in the eye to say, "Our mom died, so we live with our grandma and grandpa now. Daddy lives there too."

"I'm really sorry to hear that," Sam says to her before mouthing to me *Really sorry*.

Telling people about Lisa is never easy, but I'm especially protective of Mabel's experience. I just nod, like *I'm okay with her feelings so you can be too*. "Mabel is... processing."

I'm just gearing myself up to answer the inevitable follow-up questions when a dog's head pops up behind Sam. A very large German Shepherd, with a mouth full of very big teeth, but Mabel doesn't flinch. "Is that your dog?"

"He is," Sam says with a grin. "His name's Gomer. Do you want to say hi?"

Only then does my girl hesitate. "He's big."

Sam nods as he glances over at his dog. "He is, but he especially loves little girls."

Percy suddenly decides that he's had enough of being carried and demands to be put down. Figuring it'd be best to let him run around a little before getting on the wagon, I deposit him on the ground and follow close behind to make sure he doesn't start stomping on or pulling up strawberry plants.

When I check over my shoulder, Sam and Mabel and the dog seem to be getting along, but when Gomer gets closer to Mabel, I scoop up Percy and fly him back to the cart just in time to turn Mabel's lips away from Gomer's tongue. "Let's keep this kiss rated G, okay?"

Mabel giggles in response to the dog's slobber, but we've got limited time before Percy needs a nap, so I ask, "Can we catch a ride?"

"That's what I'm here for," Sam says, guiding us to the back of his cart, where we climb onto the hay bales lining its sides.

"Can Gomer sit by me?" Mabel asks Sam.

After I give Sam a thumbs up, Gomer hops in and settles at Mabel's feet, without a command from his master. Like he knows exactly what she needs. Once we're all in, Sam returns to the driver's seat, clucking to the horse quietly as we turn in a slow circle before heading up the hill.

As the horse lumbers along, the kids squeal at every bump in the road. There are a lot of them, but they seem to be having a blast. My arms curled around them, the sun warm on my face, the scents of dog and hay and all the farm things in my nostrils, something unwinds deep inside my chest. The three of us have had some major bumps to negotiate over the past couple of years but on this perfect summer day, all feels right in our world.

When the wagon creaks to a stop and the kids and Gomer scramble to their feet, I hop up to make sure everyone gets down safely. Sam hands each kid a small bucket and while Percy fills his with dirt, Mabel listens carefully to Sam's instructions and then proceeds to pick, murmuring *Take only the most perfect strawberries.*

Sam returns to stand next to me, Gomer sitting quietly at his side. "I really am sorry for your loss. That's tough."

Everything I feel about losing Lisa seems like the wrong thing to feel. Namely, I don't miss her, and I feel more guilty than sad about her death. But people don't want to hear any of that, so I say what's expected. "Thanks. My parents have been great, but it's obviously hard on the kids."

Sam doesn't press for more. Instead, he fills me in on his own career and life changes until his walkie-talkie squawks. He lifts it, saying, "Duty calls. Or rather, my brother's girlfriend. I need to go pick up another family. You guys want to head back down?"

I'm not ready to leave the peace of this moment, so I tell him we'll catch a ride back on his next trip. And then I plop down in the dirt with my son.

chapter
seven

AVERY

Since I haven't managed to connect with Josh in an official meeting, I've been using every free moment to jot down arguments I can make to convince him to keep Playgroup around, as well as ideas for changes to other programming at the center. By the end of the day Monday, I feel more confident about what I want to say.

But when I get home, all that goes out the window. The kitchen is a disaster area, looking like someone started and abandoned a few different recipes. That's in addition to the usual piles of unopened mail on the counter, a trash bin that needs to be emptied, and a dog whining to go out.

As I'm putting on his leash, another whimper snags my attention. In the dim light, I can just make out a human shape in the cozy nook under the bay window. My father hand-crafted the built-in bench years ago and it's been a favorite place for all of us to read or giggle with friends while my mom cooked dinner. These days, it's one of the places my mom ends up when she needs to lie down.

An impatient "woof" from the dog startles us both, but I quickly reassure my mother so she doesn't try and get up. "It's just me, Mom. I'm going to take Lenny for a quick walk. Be right back."

As our elderly Lab mix and I walk slowly around the block, I try to count my breaths like I read about on the internet, but worries about my parents and the rec center keep crowding in. It doesn't help that my mother hasn't moved by the time I get back.

"I'm sorry I didn't take the dog out," she says, her arm covering her face.

"It's fine. I needed to move after sitting on my patootie all day." Turning on the lights over the stove and counters, I ask, "Where's Dad?"

"Um, I think he's taking a nap."

I can't fix their health issues, but I can at least make sure they eat. Looking around the kitchen, I ask, "So, what were you working on for dinner here?"

My mother peeks under her elbow, like she's afraid of what she'll find. After a long moment, she shakes her head. "I'm honestly not sure."

It is so hard to see her like this. This woman raised three kids while working full-time, and never complained a day in her life. She met every challenge like it was a game, and our house was always full of people—our friends, her friends, random other people—all drawn in by her effortless hospitality.

But long-haul COVID has all but erased that person. Just like chronic pain has turned my once-hearty father into a shell of himself. I am the youngest by eight years, a classic *oops* baby, so my parents were always a little older than those of my friends. But now, they both look and behave like they're in their late eighties instead of late sixties.

I suppose it's the way of things. In the end, you take care of the people who took care of you. I get resentful sometimes that I'm the only one of my siblings doing so, but I'm also the one who moved back home with my tail between my legs.

"I'm sure I can figure something out," I say. "Do you want to go take a nap too?"

"No, it feels like I've been doing that all day. I'll just stay and talk to you if that's okay."

"Of course it is." As I take out the trash and get organized, figuring I'll just throw together a pasta dish with the vegetables my mother has half-prepped, I tell her silly stories from the day and ask her advice about a child in Playgroup.

I do *not* talk about the potential changes on the horizon.

No need to have her worrying. I can do that perfectly well on my own.

In the end, my parents end up having a decent night, both pain- and energy-wise. After dinner, we rewatch episodes of one of our favorite shows, *Parks & Recreation*. It almost feels like old times, though now it's my parents asking for "just one more" episode. Best of all, I fall asleep the minute my head hits the pillow and wake up feeling more refreshed than I have for a long time.

Before getting out of bed, I jot down additional ideas my sleeping brain came up with for programming at the center. On the short drive to CPR, I think of a few more and have to pull over twice to write them down. By the time I get to the center, I can't wait to talk to Josh Harmon.

As if the universe heard me, Wanda yells, "That Josh Harmon called for you again," as I walk past her office door.

Assuring her that I'll call him back—which I actually mean to do this time—I poke my head in Leia's office. Before I can repeat the promise to my boss, she flashes me a rare smile. "Mr. Harmon promised we will no longer be plagued by his boss's interference." The corners of her lips turn down again as she mutters, "He's just moved on to the next shiny toy, like he always did."

"Well, good." When she doesn't look up, I add, "That is good, right?"

She just shakes her head dismissively. "Josh also asked if it was okay for the grandmother to bring his son to Playgroup today. I told him it was fine."

"Of course." *Of course he wouldn't show just when I get my act together* is what I want to say, but I keep that to myself. Leia may be my bestie, but she's also my boss.

When it's time for class, the woman who enters with Percy on her hip looks less grandma, more outdoor fitness model. Her hiking shorts and boots are worn in, her face is only lightly lined, and her firm grip has me wondering if she climbs mountains as well as hikes up them. "So nice to meet you, Avery. I'm Frieda Harmon, Josh's mom. Percy just loves this playgroup, and I'm excited to try it myself."

"I'm so glad to hear that."

Her words echo in my head as I drift from child to

child, helping Theo move a bin of manipulatives, saying hello to Samar's new imaginary friend. I may not be as qualified as my mother to run the program, and it may not be the most efficient use of resources, but if Percy really loves Playgroup, maybe Josh will be open to keeping it around.

Later, as I'm pulling some books on toilet training from our little library for Theo's dad, I can't help but over-hear Mrs. Harmon's conversation with our two nosiest moms.

"He's so sweet with Percy," Inaya says, sipping her latte.

"He had a meeting this morning he couldn't miss," Frieda explains. "But this group has been so good for him. I worry sometimes that he's not doing enough to take care of his own happiness."

"I understand he has a daughter too?" Brenda asks.

"That's right. Mabel will be in first grade this fall."

While Inaya and Brenda dish the dirt on the teachers at Climax Elementary, I intervene in a conflict between Amelia and Liam. By the time I circle back, Frieda and Percy have moved across the room, leaving Inaya and Brenda to themselves.

"Can you imagine *your* husband doing what he's doing?" Inaya says in a murmur just loud enough for me to hear as I stack cups for snack time. "With my husband, the house would be a wreck, and they'd live on junk food."

"And it's so cute that the grandmother is trying to set him up with someone." Brenda sighs dramatically.

Set him up with someone? What in the actual fudge?

My thoughts are a jumble as I collect the pretzels and juice from the kitchen. Could this be true? Josh is raising his kids by himself?

Every time he's talked about Percy's mother, he's said *my wife*, not *my ex*.

Before I can even try to figure out what could be going on, a wail from the other room brings me back to the present. Shoving my thoughts to the side along with a toy bin in my way, I return to the main room and focus on the children and parents who *are* present.

After Playgroup, I have what feels like an endless to-do list to get through at my desk, so it's four o'clock by the time I grab my purse and head for my car. If I've lost my opportunity with Josh—my chance to make a case for Playgroup, not my chance to swoon over him—then I need to do everything in my power to get a second chance. I've blown off his request for a meeting so many times, I figure I need to make the effort and go to him.

As I cross the bridge over one of the rivers that flank Climax before spilling into the Hudson, I try to remember the last time I visited the southside, which has always been the industrial part of our town. Back in the eighteenth century, the area had old fashioned operations like an ice harvester and foundry. They were replaced with a shipyard and brickworks and a clock factory in the nineteenth century, but they closed one after another over the course of the twentieth century. Most of the places south of the historic district lay empty and abandoned until about thirty years ago.

An artist co-op took over one building in the nineteen nineties. A brewery, a coffee roaster, and a few restaurants came next. When the icehouse was turned into a beautiful hotel, a caterer and all kinds of wedding-related small businesses followed. I moved back in with my parents right about the time that Trede's construction signs went up, but I haven't been paying much attention to the latest change to my hometown.

When I see the complex for the first time, I get why people can't stop talking about it. Instead of razing the old brickworks and starting over, Trede transformed the factory. They even preserved some of the graffiti painted onto its sides over the years. After parking in the guest lot, I follow a walkway winding through a beautiful green-space. It's not until I come upon a map that I realize they must've filled in the quarry—the focus of complaints for years, since it was basically a dangerous hole in the ground. The leveled area now includes a dog park, water features, and native gardens.

By the time I enter the building, I feel like I've left most of my worries outside, sharp edges smoothed by the sweet scents of wildflowers, the chirping of birds, and the sparkles of sunlight reflecting off the fountains.

No wonder everyone in town wants a job here.

"Good morning. How are you today?" A person steps away from the reception desk to greet me. "I'm Van, my pronouns are they and them, and I'm so happy to welcome you to Trede."

Still in a daze, I stumble over my words as well as my feet as I respond. "Oops. Uh-um, good."

They clasp their hands together. "I love that for you."

Since they haven't asked what my business is at Trede, I return the question. "How are you?"

"I am awesome. It's a beautiful day and I'm happy to be here talking to you."

"Okay. Good. Well, I was hoping to see Josh Harmon? I don't have an appointment, but—"

"No worries." Van waves, like they're swooshing all my

cares away. Striding back to the desk, they pick up a tablet and punch in a few things. "Let me just see... Fiddlesticks! Josh is in a scrum at the moment, dealing with some bugs in the UX, but he'll probably be free in a bit."

They turn back to me, rubbing their hands together like *Have I got plans for you!* "Want a tour while you wait?"

"Oh, well, I'm not a client or a person who does... whatever it is Trede does."

Van goes hands on hips, looking affronted. "Do you live in Climax?"

"I do."

"Well, if you're a member of the Climax community"—they sweep their hands in a circle—"you're a member of our community."

"Uhhh..."

Jumping up and down, they clap like a little kid. "Come on, let's go!"

I point to the door. "What if someone comes?"

They catch the eye of an East Indian woman walking down the hall and wave at her. "Meena, I'm taking the lovely Avery on a tour."

Meena redirects her path and plops down behind the desk. "Have fun, Avery!"

As Van steers me down the hall, I crane my neck back to watch her spin in the chair. "Doesn't she have her own work to do?"

They shake their head. "We're both in OS, so it's cool."

Hopefully, I'll get some context clues because I have no idea what OS is.

Van shows me around the lower floor, split in two by an atrium filled with actual live trees, another fountain, and what looks like a self-serve snack bar. An auditorium takes up one side; the other is broken up into a meditation room, a yoga room, and a traditional gym. Except for the auditorium, every space has a view of the river.

"Being able to contemplate water is so healing," Van explains.

On the next floor, people work on computers. Some at traditional desks, others in couches or squishy chairs that look like they'd swallow you. People have dogs curled up at their feet. Fidget toys and tension balls are piled in baskets, and plants grow up trellises and hang from the ceiling.

"Would you like a milkshake?" Van asks. "We source the cow and goat and oat milks from local farms."

Before I can decline, Van gets my flavor and milk preferences, pushes a bunch of buttons on a machine, and then hands me a mocha almond freeze, which is delicious and exactly the sweet pick-me-up I didn't know I needed.

The next floor has more workspaces, plus game rooms with laser tag and nerf basketball. It's only when a man in a coat and tie lifts a plastic bag of what looks like garbage from a bin that I finally ask one of the many questions running through my mind.

"Does the janitor have to wear a tie?"

"Ken?" Van tips their head in the direction of the garbage-carrying person. "He's the director of IS. Kind of like Josh's counterpart but inward facing."

"If he's the director, why is he taking out the trash?"

Van shrugs, like *Why wouldn't he?* "Everyone takes out the trash."

They steer me around a corner into what Van calls a studio. On one end, a few people confer in front of an oversized monitor displaying what look like architectural plans. Easels face a bank of windows overlooking the river, complete with painting supplies. A backdrop, lights, and a camera on a tripod huddle together like a fancy version of a yearbook photographer's setup.

"This is my domain." Van grabs my hand and whispers, "Would you like a makeover?"

"You do makeovers? At work?"

They point to a set of mirrors surrounded by bulbs. "I do them for clients before we take their headshot photos." When I open my mouth to protest, they hold up a finger. "Whether you're a member of our globally sourced, diverse pool of entrepreneurs, or a small-town girl with sad eyes, anyone can benefit from a makeover."

As I wonder what about my eyes looks sad, they deposit me in a chair and cover me with a drape, murmuring something like, "We'll take care of that later."

"May I?" Van meets my gaze in the mirror, hands hovering over my head. When I give them the okay, they run their hands through my hair. "This color is unbelievable. Do you know what people would pay to achieve this cascade of blonds?"

They don't wait for my answer. Dropping the hair, they move on to my face, taking my chin and moving it side to side. "I wish all my clients were as faithful with their sunscreen as you obviously are."

They sigh and turn the chair so we're both facing the mirror again. "With your permission, I'd love to show you a couple makeup tips. I want to take all the beauty you've got and make it *pop*!" Their hands open like fireworks, and I can't help but get swept up in the moment.

Still, as Van starts fussing around with foundation and

blush and eye shadow palettes, I have to ask, "Don't you have, like, work to do?"

Hand on their chest, Van meets my gaze in the mirror. "Honey child, this is my life's work." They gesture around the airy room. "All of it."

As they dab my face with a cleansing wipe, Van continues. "Each person at Trede is assigned a primary role to fit their strengths—for me that's design, obvs—as well as additional roles that give them a chance to take on new challenges."

"So, what are IS and OS exactly?"

Van slaps their hands to their face *Home Alone* style. "Eek! I'm supposed to explain that. Is it obvious that giving tours is not my core competency?"

Before I can politely protest, they continue. "IS stands for Inward Service, and OS is for Outward Service. Because Trede is a pre-seed global tech builder, we balance service with growth. Our accelerator programs offer entrepreneurs the tools they need in the planning stages"—he waves a hand at the studio—"which includes all aspects of design."

Whatever any of that means, they must also be growing money. None of what I've seen could have come cheap. Before I can ask what the horse feathers a pre-seed tech builder is, however, they tell me to close my eyes and relax. "Time for me to play!"

Van's touch is gentle, and their voice is soothing, so I relax into the chair and just enjoy the experience, opening and closing my mouth and eyes as instructed, and wait to look in the mirror until they've finished.

"Ta-da!"

After Van turns the chair to face the mirror again, I

can't quite believe what I see. My skin glows, my cheeks blush, and my eyes are somehow bigger and rounder. I look exactly like myself, just... more.

"Thank you for trusting me with this gorgeous canvas." Van hands me a small cloth bag. "Product samples and instructions." They fan a set of color swatches in front of me. "This is for you to take home. I want you to throw out anything in your closet that isn't in this palette."

Before I can thank them for working their magic on me, we're interrupted by a familiar voice.

"Van! I've been looking for you. I need you to move the needle on the Pegasus group mockups. The Tiger team on that project wants to whiteboard before sending them over the wall." Eli, dressed in an outfit I bet he thinks is casual—a tie with a vest instead of a coat—turns his attention to me. "Who's your friend?

Van squeezes my shoulder and whispers, "Face blindness."

At least I'm not the only one who's invisible. "Eli, I'm Avery Mills. From Climax Parks and Rec? And from high school?"

"Of course. I didn't recognize you out of context." Tapping his head, he murmurs, "Tamagotchi."

I pause, halfway out of the chair. "Tamagotchi?"

"I apologize." He bows again, but only halfway. It's really kind of a nod. "Did I say that out loud? Because I don't recognize faces, I employ mnemonics to file people in the cache."

"What does that have to do with Tamagotchi?"

"You run children's programming at the center, and you were the girl who got people to pay her to babysit their Tamagotchi's in high school," he says, like *Duh*.

"Huh. I totally forgot about that."

"I did not." Hoping Josh will be available by now, I step away from the makeup table. "Thanks for the makeover, Van."

"My pleasure," Van says, and I actually kind of believe them.

Remembering that they'd said it was a challenge for them, I add, "Your tour was truly awesome."

"Aww, thank you!" They open their arms wide, but then freeze. "I forgot to ask first. I've learned things are different here in New York. Can I hug you?"

"Um, sure. Don't want to leave you hanging."

When their arms enclose my torso, a hiccup of emotion bubbles up. I don't think anyone has hugged me for a long time, and it feels really good. "Thanks, Van."

"Thank you, Avery." They step back and point a finger gun at Eli. "I'll go make some hay for Pegasus, Eli."

I turn to leave as well, before realizing I have no idea which way to go. "Um..."

Van has disappeared, so I ask Eli for directions back to the elevator banks, which are not at all in the direction I would've chosen. "I'm so glad you took the time to visit. I want community members to feel welcome here."

"I enjoyed the tour, but I actually came looking for Josh."

"He's been growth hacking with our new accelerator group. Doing some real blue sky thinking."

I nod, even though I have no idea what any of that means, exactly. "I was worried at first when he missed Playgroup. I'd thought maybe his wife would've brought Percy, but his mother did instead," I say, even though I doubt Eli even knows what Playgroup is.

But as I'm thinking that perhaps he does know, and that maybe he's the one—not Josh—who wants to cut the program, Eli says, "Oh no, his wife can't bring Percy anywhere. She's deceased."

The doors close between us before I can ask anything else.

Josh is not married! my girl parts sing as I head back to my car. *We're allowed to lust over him!*

But he is *a widower,* my frontal lobe warns. *He's grieving. Not a good time to get involved. For either of us.*

We could be a part of the healing process, girl parts argue, complete with a hazy, romantic movie of the two of us running toward each other in a field of flowers.

Tires screeching and the honk of a car horn bring me crashing back to reality. And into a hedge. When I try to remove myself, I end up getting tangled further. "Oh, for cod's sake!"

"Avery?" the man of my daydreams towers over me. His face is flushed, but I'm guessing it's not because he was just fantasizing about me. "You just walked in front of my car!"

The anger in his tone has me shrinking farther into the bushes. "I didn't do it on purpose. I was—" Suddenly, something below me gives way and the hedge swallows me. "Son of a bee sting!"

Josh pries apart the branches over my head. "Are you all right?"

"Yeah. Just... stuck." Wincing, I manage to disentangle one arm. "And a little scratched."

He reaches through the greenery to help me release the other arm but ends up pulling my hair. "Ow!"

"Sorry, sorry! This is like a scene from *Little Shop of Horrors*."

After several tries, we manage to free both of my hands, but my rear end is still wedged between branches. "Now what?"

"I think the only thing to do is pull you out. On three?"

When I nod, he says, "Take hold of my wrists."

I do so, and he grasps mine firmly, sending little tingles up my arms. "One, two..." we say together, but before I can say three, he hauls me out of the hedge and into his chest.

Grabbing his upper arms to keep from falling, I sputter, "You said three!"

He winces. "I was thinking the element of surprise might help."

We're nose to nose, breath puffing between us, his smelling faintly of mint. The need to know what he tastes like is stronger than my need for peanut M&Ms every afternoon at four.

His eyes rove my face, circling back to my lips. "I..." he begins, looking as discombobulated as I do. "Can I... ask you something?"

If it's *Can I kiss you?* The answer is *Oh, yes.*

Instead of saying that out loud, however, I just nod.

Eyes never leaving my lips, he sways slightly, like he was the one who just fell in a bush, or maybe fell under the spell that has me entranced. That has me closing the space between us millimeter by millimeter until... a loud honk has us both jumping back.

Son of a motherless goat!

Josh's head whips around so fast in the direction of the car horn I'm afraid it might fly right off his neck, and when he turns back to me, his eyes no longer shine with desire.

And it *was* desire, dagnabbit. It was raw need.

At least I think it was.

I step closer, but he steps back.

Okay, wait. Did I just imagine that almost-kiss? I rewind the conversation in my head. "Um, you wanted to ask me something?"

He just blinks for a few moments, so perhaps he is as flooded with hormones as I am, but then he wipes a hand down his face, wiping away all expression. "Yes. I did need to ask you something."

When he doesn't go on, I shift closer and roll my hand in the air encouragingly like *Go on*.

"Right. I needed to ask you..." He's blinking again, almost like he's clicking through options in his mind. "Oh! Yes."

I lean in just a hair farther, hoping we'll return to the immediate-post-hedge version of this convo, but then he clears his throat and blurts, "Why does Leia hate Eli so much?"

chapter
eight

JOSH

Avery steps back, sets her hands on her beautifully curved hips, and releases a heavy sigh. Like a popped balloon, she deflates before my very eyes. Or like a marionette whose puppeteer snapped its strings. Or a woman who just got asked the wrong question.

After what feels like forever, she meets my gaze again, but the light has gone out in her eyes.

Did she really want me to kiss her?

It's been a long time since a woman wanted that from me, and I'm not sure I'd recognize the signs anymore. Sad to say, I can't remember the last time I kissed Lisa before she died, other than a brief peck on the cheek. I shouldn't be thinking about any of this anyway. Especially not here in the Trede parking lot.

"That's a complicated answer," Avery finally says, her voice sounding very different than it did moments ago. "And a lot of it is personal. I'm pretty sure I don't even know the half of it, even though she's my best friend."

Avery's looking at me like it's my turn to speak, but it

takes me a few beats to remember what my question was. "I don't mean to pry. But Leia insisted that Eli stay away from the Parks and Rec department, but he seems very intent on being involved in the process."

She looks off to the side like she's considering what she can tell me, but when she bites her lip, I have to close my eyes to avoid joining in the fun. Instead, I force work words past a clenched jaw.

"The day we met, you told me they were rivals in high school and that they'd dated. If there's anything else you'd be comfortable sharing, I'd like to hear it. I need to understand their history if I'm to have a chance at convincing him to stay away."

She sighs, still gazing off somewhere past my shoulder. I've made a good argument. Saying more would likely put her off. Instead, I study her profile. Academically, of course. Her straight nose, with just a tiny little upturn at the end. The way her golden hair falls past her shoulders in a shimmery curtain. The plump lower lip captured by her top teeth as she thinks.

When she faces me again, I drop my gaze, feeling caught.

"There's one thing I could tell you, but really, I need to show you."

Hands out, palms up, I nod. "Sure, I'll take it."

She pulls her phone from her back pocket and checks it. "Do you have a half hour?"

When I nod again, she points at a car a few rows over in the guest parking lot. "Follow me."

Ten minutes later, I'm parked next to her in a downtown lot. She tips her head to the side, and I follow her quick stride toward the waterfront. Behind city hall, stately mansions perch along a road curving steeply up the cliffside. Eli's house is up there, and I wonder briefly if that's why Avery brought me here. But as I follow her down the cobblestone street, away from the fancier part of town, my gaze drops to her tantalizingly swinging hips, and the questions I really want to ask have nothing to do with our bosses. If my ability to support my kids weren't on the line, I'd say, *Forget Eli and Leia, tell me about you, Avery.*

I want to know everything from what made her want to work with kids to why she doesn't have her own children to what those lips would feel like pressed up against mine.

"So, here's the thing." She stops at the corner and points at the homes hugging the cliffs. "Millionaire's Row has always been out of reach for the middle class. They were built by the one-percenters of the time."

"Back when a millionaire was a major deal?"

"Still a pretty big deal around here. Anyway..." Turning, she leads me down a block and then back up another cobblestone street, away from the water again. This one is lined by tiny but well-crafted bungalows. "These cottages were built for factory workers. Even though they're well over a hundred years old and in need of work, the prices are out of reach for most locals. Teachers, firefighters, nurses..."

"And the director of the Parks and Recreation department?" I ask, getting where this is going.

"Right." She nods slowly, tapping her breastbone. "Program managers too. None of us can afford to live here anymore. So we're stuck in apartments near the highway, unless we want to move outside Climax to the unincorporated county."

"I get that it must be frustrating, but real estate prices have gone up all over the country." I take in the sturdy little brick homes with inviting front porches and miniature front yards. I'd say about half are under construction, and a quarter have been recently renovated. The others look like they're struggling to stand. "And at least gentrification is saving the old buildings."

Avery shoves her hands in her pockets, and I fall in step next to her as she begins to walk toward the waterfront again. Before I can ask what this has to do with Eli, she stops again and says something under her breath.

"Sorry, I missed that."

She mumbles, "It's nothing," while staring at a house the way I wish someone would look at me. Like it could make her dreams come true.

"Is that one special to you?"

"My great-great grandfather was its first owner. My family hung on to it until my grandmother died twenty years ago." Her voice is steady, but she takes a moment to swallow, like there's a lump in her throat. "I've always hoped to buy it back, but even though I put money away for a downpayment every week, I don't think I'll have enough. Unless things have changed drastically when it goes on the market again."

"Anyway." She flips a hand in the air, walking more briskly down the hill. "When Trede moved in, things got exponentially worse. These days, every single house anywhere in Climax not only gets snapped up, but bidding wars drive up the prices even higher."

"And Leia blames Eli."

"Exactly. It's also been particularly rough on her and Travis. When they split up, the kids were still really young, so they created what a lot of people thought was a crazy setup, but now it's a thing. They call it nesting."

"I've heard of that." Despite the subject matter, walking side by side with Avery is comfortable. Comforting, even. "Where the kids stay in place and the parents move in and out when it's their turn for custody?"

She nods. "They've had a little house near the rec center since the kids were born, and they also have a studio apartment nearby. But now that Trede is bringing in all these people from California and whatnot who think half a million dollars for a two-bedroom house is a bargain, one landlord wants to sell and the other's jacking up the rent. While their salaries have been frozen. So, yeah. Leia's pissed at Eli."

When she doesn't add anything else, I say, "Thank you for taking the time to tell—or show—this to me. Even though it seems like there may still be feelings between them, it'll probably be easier to get him to back off if it's about business. He's very excited about transforming Climax Parks and Rec, but hopefully these data points and the fact that we have a new crop of entrepreneurs to focus on will be enough to keep him out of your boss's hair."

The sidewalk has narrowed, so I've been following behind her. When she suddenly stops, I have to step to the side to avoid running into her. Once I've righted myself, all I can see are two perfect pink lips pressed together in a line. "I mean it, I really appre—"

She holds up a hand between us. "I know I'm supposed

to talk to you about Playgroup and all the other programming, but I need to apologize first."

"For what?"

She blows out a breath and looks up. "For... avoiding you. Being rude to you. Not returning your calls at first." Before I can accept her apology, she blurts out, "I didn't know it was about work stuff. I thought you were hitting on me."

"Um, well. For the record, I do need to discuss Parks and Rec programming with you..." It's a bad idea—a very bad idea—but that doesn't stop me from blurting out the truth. "But I also can't stop thinking about you. What it would be like to kiss you."

Her cheeks pink up, but she meets my gaze. "For the record, I've wondered that too. Since you first helped me pick up those art supplies."

"Then why were you avoiding me?"

"Because I thought you were taken." She points at my left hand. "You're wearing a ring."

"Oh. Right." I lift my hand and stare at my wedding ring. The one I've taken off and put back on many times over the past year and a half.

"Eli told me today that you're a widower. I'm sorry for your loss." She tucks her hands in her back pockets. "Is that why you still wear the ring? Because you're still grieving?"

"It's not so much that, it's... it's just easier to wear it, because, I mean, I am..." *How to say this?* "Taken. By my kids."

"Is... all of you taken?" Avery steps closer, and all I can focus on are her gray-blue eyes, the color of a gathering storm. Until she trails a finger over my jaw and every brain cell rushes to meet her touch. "I mean, what about this part?"

"That's... available." My throat's somehow too full of my heart to get much sound out but when her mouth replaces her fingertip, I think it might explode.

"And this?"

Her lips skate to the spot between my jaw and my ear and I manage something like, "Yeah, um, that's wide open too."

Her warm breath hovers over the corner of my mouth as she whispers, "Is anyone using this these days?"

"You," I growl, grasping her jaw in my hands and pulling her mouth to mine. "Just you." A gentle brush of my lips over hers quickly morphs to a demand for more. To explore every inch of her mouth, inside and out. My hands can't get enough of her hair, even silkier than I'd imagined. When we stumble into a tree, every hard place in me meets all her softness as I press her into its trunk.

I'd worry that it's too much, but she pulls me even closer. I'm echoing her needy moans and whimpers with groans, and I can barely tell where she begins, and I end. The tolling of a bell resonates through our bodies. When it happens again, Avery freezes. On the third peal, she shoves me away and staggers back.

Eyes wild, she looks everywhere but at me. "I, uh, have to go."

The next morning, I'm still reeling from that interrupted kiss. Confused about why Avery literally sprinted away from me, of course. But also thrown by how the kiss made me feel.

Before my kids were born, I kind of assumed that I was just the kind of person who didn't feel anything deeply. That I was just an even-tempered guy. I'd always had plenty of friends and could always find something to like about pretty much every person I met. I figured it was a good thing that I didn't suffer from heartbreak like other people or get into fights or get my feelings hurt.

I mean, I wondered what it must feel like to fall deeply in love, but it wasn't like I missed something I'd never felt.

Until the moment I held Mabel in my arms. The rush of emotions totally blindsided me. I knew I'd die for her. Or kill for her. Her safety and happiness made all the things I'd valued before seem insignificant.

I'd hoped that Mabel might bring Lisa and me closer, that my feelings for my wife might deepen. That I was learning how to be in love. Instead, it was like Lisa and I traded places at that moment. Suddenly, she couldn't wait to get back to work and I could barely make myself leave the house because I resented the time I had to be away from my daughter.

It happened all over again with Percy. The wallop of falling in love with my son even as the gap between my wife and me widened. As a result, I figured that while I am capable of some deep feelings, I'm just not made for romance.

Until last night.

The attraction between Avery and me has been obvious since the moment she dropped those boxes, revealing those big blue eyes, set so perfectly in her heart-shaped face, framed by hair that is as soft and inviting as the rest of her. I've loved watching her with the kids in Playgroup and admired her deft handling of squabbles, whether they're between children or parents.

But the moment our lips met, something else happened.

Part instinctive, almost-animalistic urge, part soul-baring need, the drive to fuse my entire self with her was so strong, I don't know what I would've done if that bell hadn't startled me back to reality.

"Can I help you?"

Crashing down to earth all over again, it takes me a moment to figure out where I am. Which means I navigated my way to the mayor's office completely on autopilot. Hopefully, no one was harmed in the process.

I smile at the receptionist looking at me like I've been staring off into space for far too long. "Um, yes. Sorry. I have an appointment. Josh Harmon from Trede?"

"Oh, yes of course, Mr. Harmon. I didn't place you without the others. She'll see you in a moment."

Every other meeting with the mayor of Climax has included Eli and his usual entourage as well as myself, and I do try to melt into the background in order to most efficiently observe and strategize. From previous meetings I've determined that the mayor of Climax—a shrewd woman, perhaps battle-scarred from having to fight for every penny—obviously cares about the town she serves. Since I need to finalize a few things with the administration before we can move forward with the next phase of the Parks and Rec plan, I'm curious to see what it'll be like to work with her one-on-one.

Moments later I'm sitting across from Martina Diaz, a woman who could be anywhere from forty to sixty.

Diaz always looks like she expects to be disappointed, but when I make it clear that I'm here to get things done, her smile shifts from wary to complicit. In minutes, she's connected me with the city employees and contractors with whom I'll need to interface, and I have her okay to move forward with the next phase of the project.

As she's walking me out, the clock bell tolls. Suddenly on fire from the memory of the last time it rang, I pull at the collar of my shirt before checking my watch, just to make sure that I won't be late for my next meeting. What I see stops me in my tracks. "What is up with that clock, anyway? It's ten twenty-two. Not the top of the hour or even the quarter."

"You haven't visited the gift shop?" Mayor Diaz asks, her Brooklyn accent making her out-of-context question sound like an accusation.

"Gift shop?" Before she can explain, I add, "Can't the owner fix it?"

"Not unless they want to give the money back."

"What money? And who are they?"

"A large sum of money was bequeathed to the city by the clock's creator, including an endowment for the maintenance of the entire waterfront." The mayor gestures toward the bank of windows overlooking the Hudson. Outside, people stroll down the boardwalk past well-kept planters and comfortable-looking benches. "People walk along the river, they stop for a drink or an ice cream or to browse in one of the little shops..."

"The waterfront is an amenity that the town values. That makes sense."

"Exactly."

"But why does the clock ring at random times? Is it some kind of mindfulness thing?"

"Depends on who you ask." Hands behind her back, she moves closer to the windows, and I follow. "And whether you believe the answer."

"What's there to believe?"

"Supposedly, the bell tolls when someone's falling in love."

"How the hell would it know that?"

Her knowing smirk makes it clear that she sees right through me and my besotted heart. "Have you ever heard of an Ormolu clock?"

Again, not what I was expecting to hear. "I... no, I have not."

"Okay, well," she begins, and then proceeds to tell a long and winding tale about Climax Clocks and its founder Klaus something-or-other. "He had what they used to call Mad Hatter's disease."

"Oh, like that guy in the *S-Town* podcast? They think he died of mercury poisoning from restoring clocks?"

"Yes, like that guy," she says with a huff. "Anyway, *creating* the Ormolu clocks was just as dangerous as fixing them. Something to do with how they applied the gold paint. Anyway, he was some sort of genius, but also not quite right in the head. He said that when two people kiss or"—she breaks off, her neck and chest turning as pink as her cheeks—"um, you know..."

"Climax?"

She snorts. "Yeah. That. He claimed that he created an instrument that could detect some sort of vibrations that are emitted when soulmates, uh, come together."

"And that sets off the clock?"

"That's the legend. If the bell tolls, someone's found their one true love."

Is that what happened last night? Is Avery my one true love? I let this line of thought go for about forty-two seconds before chastising myself. I may read my kids fairy tales, but I don't believe in them.

Thankfully, the mayor is gazing out the window, a dreamy look on her face. "Somewhere in Climax, someone fell in love at ten twenty-two this morning."

"Did he?"

"He who?" She blinks for a moment before looking over at me. "Klaus Clijsters?"

"Right. The clock guy. Did he fall in love?"

The corners of her lips lift slowly as she gazes at the bell tower. "He did, actually. According to the book in the gift shop, anyway."

"At least he had a happy ever after."

She turns back to me with a wince. "Well, only for a couple of years. I think they both died horrible deaths from mercury poisoning."

"Oh."

"You want to know what's worse? Up until a few years ago, the gift shop did a lovely job selling the romance. But just when local businesses busted out romantic hotel packages and restaurant menus all centered around the clock, that darn podcast took off and now, all anybody wants to talk about is the similarity to the clock guy in *S-Town*." She shakes her head. "That is not the image we were hoping for."

chapter
nine

AVERY

It's silly to believe that a clock can detect true love, even if the guy who created it was supposedly a genius. And no one really agrees on what the tolling of the bell means anyway. Climax kids love to scare each other with Klaus Clijsters ghost stories, claiming that when the bell rings, he sees whatever naughty thing you're up to. Mayor Diaz has pushed the true love legend, but most reasonable Climaxians recognize that story for what it truly is: a marketing angle.

It's just a broken clock, and I should be thankful that its random clanging kept me from embarrassing myself. Even if I haven't been able to stop thinking about that kiss since the moment I walked—or possibly ran—away from Josh.

Just because it was the hottest kiss I've ever experienced does not mean that he and I are meant to be together. He's a widower who is probably still grieving, for fork's sake. He has two children he needs to focus on. He probably wouldn't be interested in anything other than a fling, and I can't afford to get my heart broken all over again.

Apparently, I haven't entirely convinced myself that I should ignore all signs pointing to Josh because the minute I get to work, I stick my head into Leia's office and blurt, "Have you ever had the Climax Clock go off on you?"

I'm surprised when she instantly answers in the affirmative, but before I can ask for details, she snorts and adds, "But that relationship didn't last, so the clock's love legend is obviously a fairy tale."

Before she can ask why I'm asking, I make an excuse and hightail it to my office. But the moment my seat hits my office chair, I find a hole in her logic. Travis and Leia may not have stayed married for long, but they will be connected forever by their twins. So maybe the clock does know when two people are fated to share their lives.

It just doesn't say how.

Or maybe you have to do the work to make the fairy tale come true.

The next day, when Wanda buzzes me with a call from Josh Harmon, I take it. But instead of asking about children's programming or addressing the kiss I can't stop thinking about, he asks, "I don't suppose CPR has any sudden openings in its day camp?"

There's worry in his tone, and I immediately switch to problem solving mode. "We do, but Percy's a little young. The cutoff is five."

"I wasn't asking for Percy. My daughter Mabel is six.

Things have been so bad at the camp she's been going to that they gave up and refunded my money."

"Oh no. What happened?"

"It's not Mabel, at least not in any bad way. I think it was just a poor fit. To me it sounded great. It's just outside of town and they have all these outdoor activities like fishing and rock climbing. But for her, it was one disaster after another, from getting hives after being stung by a bee to getting a fish hook stuck in her thumb. All topped off by some mean girl drama."

My heart squeezes in sympathy for the little girl. "Poor thing."

"When I checked earlier in the summer, CPR's camp was full. But you have openings now?"

"Our prices are much lower than the private camps, so we fill up fast. But at the end of August, there's a big drop off when the summer people go back to Manhattan or Albany or wherever." I click open our current camp roster. "You said Mabel is six?"

Clicking between the upcoming week's staff list and the camper list tells me that it'll be tight, but of course I can't say no. "We lost some of our college-aged counselors, but I could take one little girl who sounds like she needs a positive camp experience."

"The thing is, she's just not outdoorsy. Or athletic, really."

"Got it. She'll be on the Leia track, then." I create a record for Mabel and begin to copy and paste contact info from Percy's.

"Leia as in the CPR director?"

"Yes, but it's not like she's a counselor or anything. Before kids start camp, they rank the activities by interest.

For the most part, I find they divide themselves in two groups. I call them Leias and Travises. Leias are mostly indoors doing imaginative or learning activities; Travises are mostly outside playing sports. I say mostly because I make the Leias go outside for some fresh air and the Travises come inside for a break."

"What do the Leias do?"

"I'm going to send you a questionnaire to fill out when we hang up, so you'll see what's offered, but it depends on the skill sets of the summer hires. Like, this year we have improv and puppetry; last year we had drumming. But there's always art, crafting, library visits, puzzles, board games... things like that."

"What do you teach?"

"Oh, I don't teach. I'm the administrator."

"But you teach Playgroup."

"That's just because it was my mom's program, and I'd helped her out a lot over the years. So when we needed someone to take over, I was the best candidate. Even though I really have no business doing it."

"Why? You're great at it."

"That's kind of you to say, but I'm not a parent, nor did I study child development. I just have my mom's notes. And I've done a lot of research since I took it on," I add, to make sure he knows I'm not just winging it. And it was a gradual process, really. I went from assisting my mom with any heavy lifting, to subbing occasionally when she didn't feel well, to taking over the class because she just didn't have it in her anymore.

"I'm sorry to hear about your mom. Is she..." He lets the question hang in the air, but there's an empathetic wince in his tone.

"She's still with us, just not her old self." That's as much information as I usually share. My mom's pretty private about her diagnosis. But something makes me add, "She has chronic COVID."

If I hadn't been living with them, I doubt they would've figured out that it wasn't just menopause slowing my mom down. If I didn't have such a flexible schedule, where I could drive my mom to Hudson, and then Albany as we tried to figure out what was causing her extreme fatigue and depression, it would've been even harder to get the diagnosis, or what passes for one since there's no real test. At least she's eligible for disability, but it doesn't make living with the condition any less tricky.

"I'm sorry to hear that. I knew several people with it back in the city. It's a tough thing to live with."

"It is," I agree, thinking how, even now, it's hard to tell if her anxiety is a result of long-haul COVID or the fact that she can't do all the things she used to. "My dad lives with chronic pain, so there were times I'd come home from work to find them both still in bed."

"So you live with your parents too?"

"I do. They need the help and I'm the only one of my siblings left in town." His wording takes a moment to hit home. "Are you saying that you live with your parents?" He's so accomplished and put together, it's hard to imagine him moving back home.

"For me, it's because *I* need the help. I couldn't have gone back to work full time without them." He clears his throat. "So your camp. It sounds perfect for Mabel. When can she start?"

I spend the rest of the week and the entire weekend berating myself for the pickle I've gotten myself into. I may have successfully fixed his daughter's day camp problem, but neither he nor I managed to bring up his plans for CPR programming. Not to mention that possibly fateful kiss. Considering the number of times I replayed the encounter over the weekend, I doubt I'll ever be able to talk to him about anything in person without wanting to kiss him again, as unprofessional as that is.

What can I say? The bell made me do it?

Monday morning, I'm trying this argument on for size when my office phone rings. It takes me a moment to shake off the lust haze enough to answer. "This is Avery."

"Ms. Mills?"

Nobody calls me Ms. Mills. Even the kids call me Miss Avery. And I don't recognize the older male voice. "This is she."

"I'm so sorry to bother you. This is Bert Harmon. Josh's dad?"

"Oh, hello. How are you?"

"Well, I've been better. Again, I'm so sorry to call you like this but we don't know many people in town yet and we've got a small problem."

"No worries. How can I help?"

"Well, Frieda—that's my wife—has broken her ankle."

"Oh my goodness. Is she okay?"

"She'll survive." Something crashes in the background. "Percy's with us at Urgent Care, and you can imagine how that's going."

As if on cue, I hear a familiar squeaky voice shout out, "Pussy!"

"Yep, that's you buddy," Mr. Harmon says. "So, the other part of the problem is, Josh is in New York for the day, and I haven't been able to get him on the phone. Even if I do, it's at least a couple hours on the train to get back here."

"Do you want me to come get Percy?"

"I know you're probably at work and it's an imposition but—"

"It's no problem. I'm just doing paperwork. I can swing by and pick him up and he can hang out here for the rest of the afternoon. You probably know that Mabel started camp here last week."

"It actually might be more than just the afternoon." As he talks, I shut down my computer and scrawl a *Be Back Soon* note, which I pin to my door. "The break is bad enough that the doctor here thinks she needs surgery, which means we've got to drive to the hospital in Albany."

"Oh, dear. That sounds awful." Grabbing my keys and my bag, I pull my office door shut and head for my car.

"They gave her something for the pain and the ankle is stabilized but she's pretty uncomfortable."

"I'll be there in ten minutes. You just take care of Mrs. Harmon."

Twenty minutes later, Mr. Harmon and I have moved the car seats from his car to mine and I've got Percy buckled in with one of those cheap little toys they hand out at doctors' offices, a squishy ball already covered in drool. "Looks like somebody's teething."

"He is. There are some little drops in the side pocket if he gets fussy." Mr. Harmon sets a large diaper bag on the front seat. "I hope I'll be back before dinner, but just in case, keys to the house and the address are also in there."

"Keep me posted, but don't worry. I can stay until Josh gets back."

"I finally got ahold of him, and he said he'd catch the next train, so hopefully it won't be too long."

Back at the rec center, Percy plays while I work on my laptop, happy to have all the toys to himself. Near the end of the day, I get a text from Mr. Harmon letting me know that they made it to the hospital but are still waiting for the surgery. I tell him not to worry, and after checking in with my parents and letting them know that I'm babysitting for a friend, I tell Percy we're going to play with the big kids and go in search of Travis. As expected, I find him inside the humid, funky-smelling gym, watching the twelve-year-old campers do some sort of basketball drill.

"Hey, Travis. Can I get you to watch this little guy for a few minutes?"

Before I can explain who he is, Travis opens his arms wide. "Pussy, my man!"

Percy wiggles and leans toward Travis, so I hand him over.

"High five, Pussy!" Percy's tiny hand is dwarfed by Travis's, but he smacks it with all his might. "Good one."

"I'll be back in fifteen," I promise.

"No worries," Travis says before blowing his whistle. "Pussy can help me put the balls away."

Checking my watch and running through the camper schedule in my head, I hustle to the art room, where Daisy has the six-year olds for the final period of the day. Thankful that I checked in on Mabel enough during her first week at camp that she'll know who I am, I pop my head in Daisy's room. "Can I borrow Mabel for the rest of the afternoon?"

Daisy shoots me an *Everything okay?* look, which I return with a reassuring nod.

"We'll be working with the stamps again tomorrow, Mabel," Daisy says. "So you can finish then."

"I'm already finished, Miss Daisy." Mabel hands over a piece of paper covered with colorful splotches.

While Daisy hangs up her artwork to dry, Mabel meets me at the door. "Do you need me to help with the snacks again, Miss Avery?"

As I usher her out, careful to avoid touching her since I'd noticed her flinching away from a counselor's reach on her first day, she says, "Oh, but it's not snack time."

"You're right, it's almost pickup time," I say as I lead her down the hall toward my office.

"Am I in trouble?"

Her tone is more curious than worried, like she's working her way through all the possibilities in her head.

"Not that I know of. Did you do something naughty?"

I glance over and have to stifle a laugh as I watch her seriously consider the question. "Not today."

Opening my office door, I gesture for her to enter. "You can tell me about that later, if you'd like, but right now, I need to tell you about a change in plans for your family." Sitting in the guest chair by my desk so that I'm eye level with her, I say, "Your grandma had an accident this afternoon."

She blinks rapidly for a few moments before asking, "Is she dead?"

"No, no, honey. She's fine. She's going to be fine." It takes everything I've got to keep myself from wrapping her in a hug. What must it be like to have experienced the death of a parent at her age? To be constantly worried that other people in your life will die too? "She fell and hurt her ankle, and your grandpa called me to pick up Percy and I'm going to hang out with both of you until your dad gets back from New York."

She nods, like she's tucking this information away for safekeeping. When she asks where Percy is, I take her to the gym. She declines to enter, declaring that it's too stinky. After I collect her brother and bundle both kids into my car, I get her talking about camp during the drive home.

After Mabel punches in the lock code, the children give me a quick tour of the house. We start upstairs, where Mabel shows me her tidy room, proudly showing off all the books she can read as well as her many art supplies and projects. Percy takes me by the hand and pulls me to his room, where he introduces me to his favorite stuffed animals and trucks. I'm doing my best not to wonder where Josh sleeps, when Percy declares that he's "hungy."

Back downstairs, Mabel tells me what they like to eat. The kitchen is bright and homey and well organized, with kid art stuck to cabinets, a bowl of fruit on the island, and a perfect little breakfast nook overlooking the backyard. I get Percy set up in his high chair with a banana while I put together a quick dinner from what's in the fridge.

After I get the beans warming and the quesadillas browning, I glance over at Percy, who's managing to get about half of the banana into his mouth, while he uses the other half to make patterns on his tray.

"Nana boo-boo."

I've gotten pretty good at Percy-speak over the past

few weeks, so I get that he means his grandmother had an accident. "She did."

"Owie."

"She does have an owie. But the doctor will make it better."

"Wheh dada?" Percy asks, looking around suddenly.

"He's on the way." He doesn't seem upset, but just in case, I divert his attention. "Do you want milk or water to drink?"

"Mik," Percy says.

"I'll get it," Mabel says, jumping down from the table where she's been quietly coloring.

"Thanks for being so helpful, Mabel. I'd be lost without you."

"I know." Mabel pulls a sippy cup from a drawer and carefully fills it and a small cup with milk. "But you have to feed the cat. The food is too stinky for me."

After I cut up the quesadillas into wedges and serve them with chunks of avocado on top, Mabel tells me where the cat food is.

I look around the kitchen. "But where's the cat?"

"She'll come when she hears you. She's shy."

As I open the can, Mabel pinches her fingers over her nose. "Yuck!"

"It is kind of stinky." The moment I set the dish on the counter, a tiny black cat appears out of nowhere. "Aww. She's adorable."

After I join the kids at the table, I ask, "What's her name?"

"Jenny Linksy."

"Like in *Jenny and the Cat Club*?"

Mabel nods enthusiastically. "They're my favorite books."

"They were mine too."

Her brows come together like I've disappointed her. "Not anymore?"

"Well, I'm not sure. I've read a lot of books since I was your age."

Her lips twist to the side for a moment, but then she says, "Fair."

As Mabel and I clear the table, both the cat and Percy get the zoomies, running in circles around the adjoining great room. I follow Mabel's instructions for bathtime and the rest of their evening routines, managing to get Percy down just as he starts to get fussy. When Mabel and I snuggle in bed to read together, the cat crawls onto my lap. I scratch under her chin, and she purrs loudly.

"Jenny Linsky is afraid of most people," Mabel says. "But she likes you."

"Maybe because I like her."

We take turns reading a couple of the Esther Averil classics featuring the little black cat adopted by a sea captain. Mabel's reading ability seems to be pretty advanced for her age. Either that, or she has the books completely memorized. As I climb out of the bed and turn off the lamp, the moment feels bittersweet. I always tell myself that I'm happy to hand off the kids I work with to their parents at the end of the day, but if I'm honest with myself, I'd love to have this every night with children of my own.

If that were possible.

Pushing those thoughts to the side, I tuck the covers

under Mabel's chin. "Thanks again for your help today. You're a very good big sister."

"I know," she says on a sigh so heavy it's almost comical. "Do you have any brothers?"

I've babysat enough that I recognize a question meant to put off bedtime, but I answer anyway, telling her that I have an older brother and sister, that I'm the baby of the family.

"So I'm kind of, like, older than you," she says.

Grinning at her logic, I turn toward the bedroom door just as a tall, dark figure steps through it. I open my mouth to scream but Mabel beats me to it.

chapter
ten

JOSH

There's nothing like a meeting with my in-laws' attorneys to tank my faith in humanity. As I exit the conference room on the top floor of the steel and glass monolith that houses the Kingston family enterprises, I'm truly thankful I had a lawyer friend look over the prenup I signed before marrying Lisa Kingston.

Otherwise, I'm pretty sure I'd be handing over my children as well as the keys to our old apartment today. I mean, yeah, I was depressed after Lisa died. Yes, I quit my job. But it was to take care of my fucking kids, not lie around and live off of Lisa's life insurance.

Lisa's parents think every problem can be solved by throwing money at it. I may not be any good at romantic relationships, but I know in my bones that I'm a better parent than either of them ever were to my wife. They gave her every so-called advantage, from a Mandarin tutor to a personal shopper, but they did not give her unconditional love.

Control freaks that they are, it drives them crazy that

I've moved the kids up to what they call "that tiny town in the middle of nowhere." I may have judged Climax at first, but now, their opinion only bolsters my conviction that moving was the right thing to do. Away from the pressures of growing up in Manhattan, where parents scrabble to get their precious offspring accepted by the best private schools when they're practically in the womb. Public school was good enough for me, and it'll be good enough for Mabel and Percy.

The much-too-long meeting with the attorneys confirmed one thing for sure. I have no business thinking I can make something work with Avery. I'm oh-for-one in the romance arena and I need to keep it that way. My kids have had enough trauma for one lifetime. I don't need to add a breakup to it.

No matter what the damn clock says.

Unfortunately, that was only the appetizer. Lisa's parents have also requested—aka demanded—that I have dinner with them while I'm in town. As if I'd be in town for any other reason than their summons. Needing fresh air before the next ordeal, I push through the revolving doors and step onto the sidewalk. The reflection of the late afternoon sunlight off the surrounding office buildings blinds me momentarily but when I'm able to see my phone screen, I realize I've missed quite a few calls.

Almost all from my father.

When I hear his recorded voice say, "Your mother had an accident," I almost drop the phone. Fingers numb, hands shaking, I crush the damn thing against my ear to the point of pain so I don't miss a word, even though my chest feels like it's caving in on itself.

Stumbling toward the intersection, I somehow hail a

cab and say something about getting me to Penn Station. Listening to the rest of the voicemails as we crawl through traffic—wishing Scotty could just beam me the fuck up so I could get to my family—is torture. By the time I hear the last message, I know that my dad arranged for someone to stay with the kids, that he and my mom made it to Albany, and that my mom will soon go into surgery.

I can breathe, but that's about it. I have no idea who has the kids, where they are, or how my mom is doing. And now my dad isn't answering *his* phone.

On the northbound train, after leaving a message with Lisa's parents to cancel dinner, I check work emails, but it's impossible to focus. Since I can't fix what's happening in Climax, my mind keeps circling back to what I did wrong with Lisa. Wondering if I could've made her happier. We'd only been dating for a couple months when that condom broke and she ended up pregnant. She was all about her career, so I fully expected her to end the pregnancy. But I guess hormones are powerful things because she decided to keep the baby, whether I stuck around or not. She floated through those nine months, climbing the corporate ladder by day and reading every parenting book there was by night.

But it was like a light switched off after we brought Mabel home. Having to recover from an unexpected Caesarean probably didn't help, but Lisa quickly relinquished care for our little girl to the nanny, convinced that a professional was better equipped than we'd ever be.

After that, we both just went back to work.

I wish I'd known more about postpartum depression, including the fact that it can last for years. Wish I'd pressed her to talk to her doctor about it sooner. Once she did, I wish I'd pushed harder for her to keep up therapy. But the minute Mabel started preschool, Lisa decided she wanted another baby, and when Lisa decided something, it was nearly impossible to change her mind. She argued that she'd do better the second time around. And she did spend more time with Percy as an infant, as did I. Breastfeeding was easier, and he was a good sleeper. Things were better all around. Or so I thought.

Until she stepped in front of a bus.

The police declared the incident an unfortunate accident. But I still wonder whether or not she did it on purpose.

By the time I pull into the driveway of my parents' house, I'm spiraling. I adore my kids, but—as is often the case for children who've lost a parent early in life—they do not handle change well. Last-minute, unexpected change is especially hard.

When I enter the house, it's eerily quiet. No screaming, no tantrums. There are dishes in the sink and backpacks at the table, but no other signs of life. At the top of the stairs, I peek inside Percy's room and find him sound asleep, clutching his favorite blanket, thumb stuffed in his mouth. After giving him a kiss on the forehead, I head for Mabel's room. Her door is ajar too, but there's a light on inside.

As I get closer, I recognize Mabel's voice. I can't understand what she's saying but she sounds calm enough. When I peek inside, I witness something I honestly thought I'd never see again: my daughter being happily tucked in by someone other than me or her grandparents.

"Daddy!" Mabel squeals.

Avery screams, her hand going to her heart. "Good gravy! You scared the shish kebobs out of me."

Mabel jumps up and pulls me over to sit down on her bed before snuggling back under the covers next to the woman I thought I'd convinced myself to let go of. She's all Miss Avery this and Miss Avery that, while Avery quietly blows Mabel a kiss good night, saying that she'll be downstairs.

By the time I get my daughter settled and return to the kitchen, Avery is closing the dishwasher. Instead of dropping to my knees and thanking her for everything she's done, I ask, "What are you doing here?"

"I didn't just waltz in here," Avery shoots back. "Your dad called me because they didn't know what else to do."

Scrubbing my hands over my face, I groan. "I'm sorry. I got this series of panicked messages, then one saying they got the kids squared away, not to worry, but..."

"You were worried."

"Yeah."

"Have you heard anything about how the surgery went?"

Shaking my head, I check my phone again. "Oh, there's a text from my dad now." Reading quickly through it, I blow out a sigh. "She's out of surgery, in recovery, everything went fine. He's going to stay at a hotel in Albany since it's so late and drive back tomorrow."

"I'm glad she's okay."

"It is a relief." I look around at the kitchen, which Avery has straightened up in addition to doing the dishes. On top of making dinner for my kids and caring for them at the drop of a hat. "Anyway, I'm sorry if my dad imposed on you. Maybe it's time to find some childcare backup."

"Not an imposition at all. We had a great time."

The adrenaline that's been coursing through my body since I got the first message that there'd been an accident —eerily similar to the one I got when Lisa was killed— suddenly drains away. I can actually feel it leaving my bloodstream, and I suddenly feel like I could sleep for a week.

"Well, I guess I'll just head out," Avery says.

Blinking heavily, it takes me a moment to realize that she's at the kitchen door, bag over her shoulder. I follow, intending to walk her to her car, but when she turns around, I end up grasping her shoulders to keep from plowing her over.

Aaand we're right back where we were a week ago. Knowing I shouldn't, I let my hands skate down her arms and lean down until I can feel her breath tease my lips. Hovering there, I give her the opportunity to bail, but she meets me instead.

"Thank god," I mutter between urgent kisses. "I was worried that I'd never get to do this again."

She doesn't say anything, just wraps her arms around my neck and threads her fingers into the hair at my nape. My hands continue to roam, needing to feel as much of her as I can. When I palm her butt cheeks and squeeze, she moans into my mouth, the vibration reverberating down to my toes.

"If things were different," I murmur, running my fingers through cornsilk hair.

"What would you do?" She presses closer, breasts I'm dying to caress flattening against my chest. "If things were different?"

"I wouldn't let you leave."

"How deeply do your kids sleep?" she whispers.

Shit. I completely forgot about my kids. Which is why this is such a bad idea. Stepping away feels wrong, but my frontal lobe—for better or for worse, I'm honestly not sure at this moment—takes over and I force my body away from hers. "Not deeply at all."

An expression I can't quite identify crosses her face, but before I can say anything that would make her feel better, she nods briskly. "I'll see you in class, then."

Before she makes it out the door, however, she slaps her forehead. "Oh fudge. The car seats are still in my car."

We make it out the door without kissing or colliding again, but it takes everything in me to stay away from her perfectly rounded ass as she wiggles and twists her torso into the back seat of her two-door sedan. "How'd you even get them in there?"

When she re-emerges with the booster seat, she's laughing, like the last eight hours have been a fun adventure for her, rather than a total pain in the ass. "There was some colorful swearing from your dad, to be sure. I think he owes Mabel about twenty bucks."

As I take it from her, I do my best to focus on her words rather than the inviting lips they issue from. "So, um, what is it with you and the fake curse words, anyway?"

She laughs again, a sound so soft and inviting, I want to clutch it to me like Percy's blankie. "Believe me, I used to swear like a sailor. Especially when I got mad."

I have a hard time picturing either of those things, but I just ask, "What changed?"

Her expression shifts, but in the dim light it's hard to read. "My mom really needed me to take over Playgroup, but she was worried about what she called my 'potty mouth.'"

"So you just quit? Like cold turkey?"

She snorts. "Believe me. It was as hard as I can imagine quitting smoking would be."

I lean closer. "So a four-letter word never passes your lips?"

"I'd say I'm in control of it." Lips I want to taste again twist in a crooked grin. "Ninety-nine percent of the time, anyway."

Now all I can think of is making her lose that control, but that cannot happen in my parents' driveway, so I just nod and gesture to her car door. "Do you want me to unhook Percy's? Those things can be tricky, in all fairness to my dad."

"Nah, I got it." She waits a beat, like maybe she's struggling too, before reaching in to release the car seat like she does this every day.

"You have no idea how amazing it is that you know how to deal with these things when you don't even have kids."

We trade seats so I have Percy's larger one, and she follows me to the garage. "You should see me change a diaper."

"I have." After stowing the seats and Percy's bag by the steps, I thank her again.

"Anytime. Seriously. Your kids are fun."

I walk her back to her car, open the door, and take a deep breath. "Think the bell would chime if I kissed you again?"

She hesitates a fraction of a second before stepping

close. "Nobody knows what's going to happen tomorrow. Why not enjoy today?"

I nod, even as I say, "I just don't want anyone to get hurt. Especially my kids."

"Eh, even if you turn out to be a jerk, I'd be nice to your kids."

"You promise?"

"I do."

Leaning over the top of the car door, I press my lips to hers. When they part, I'm lost in the feel of her, the slick of skin on skin. Until I hear the peal of a bell in the distance.

Breaking the kiss, my heart thudding hard, I whisper, "Did you hear that?"

She shudders, but it's hard to tell if it's a good thing or a bad thing. "I did."

My hand trembles as I reach for hers, but when I clasp it, everything calms. "I'll be honest, Avery. I have a hard time seeing past next week, and my life is not my own. But you make me want... more."

She bites her bottom lip and traces a finger over my thumb. "I know what you mean."

After a long moment where we just nod at each other, followed by mirrored goofy smiles, she sighs and disentangles us. I watch as she settles in the driver's seat, starts the car, and backs out of the driveway. I keep watching until her taillights disappear around the corner, needing to hold on to this feeling. Like she's unspooling a thread between us even as she drives away from me. My attraction to Avery is off the charts, but there's something else too. A connection that tugs at my heart. That has me wondering if I'm falling in love.

For the very first time.

chapter
eleven

AVERY

There's something about the way that Josh looks at me that has lit a fire in my belly.

I'm a little afraid of it burning out of control, but I'm not ready to douse it either. Kissing him is so good that I can't stop wondering what else he might be good at. It was not an easy feat to keep such naughty thoughts packed away during Playgroup this morning, especially when Josh tossed Percy up in the air, making his muscles bulge deliciously while the little boy giggled adorably.

Now, while I plug away at data entry for CPR's fall classes, my imagination replaces Percy with my torso and shifts Josh from his feet to his back. I'm straddling him and he drags his hands from my rib cage to my breasts. When he pinches my nipples between his thumbs and forefingers, I grind into him greedily.

"You going to answer that?" Leia yells from inside her office.

"Yep!" I call, blinking back to reality. "Just had to finish... this." Not that I actually finished anything. That'll have to happen later. In my bed. With my favorite vibrator.

"This is Avery," I say after snatching up the phone before it can ring again, my voice a little breathless.

"Hello, Avery. This is Frieda Harmon. How are you?" Josh's mom asks.

"I'm fine, thanks, but how are *you*?" It's been several days since the accident, and Josh told me that his mom had returned from the hospital, but in the crush of Playgroup, I didn't get many details.

After assuring me that she's on the mend, she says, "I understand that neither my husband nor my son paid you for babysitting Mabel and Percy the other day."

Suddenly the make out session outside their house feels even more like teenagers sneaking around. But if I'm the babysitter, who is Josh in this scenario? The dad or my boyfriend who came over when he wasn't supposed to?

"Are you still there?"

"Oh yes, I'm sorry, Mrs. Harmon."

"Please call me Frieda, honey."

"Sure, um, Frieda. Anyway, I was just being a good neighbor. You don't have to pay me for that."

"If it were an hour, I'd agree. But you took responsibility for my grandchildren for almost eight hours. Please let me do something to show our appreciation."

"Really, it's not—"

"What, dear? I'm sorry, Avery. My husband is saying something. Oh, that's a good idea. He said we should give you a gift certificate. Is there a place where you get your nails done?"

I laugh. "I'm afraid manicures don't last long at my job."

"There must be something you've been wanting to splurge on. How about a restaurant? Treat yourself to a nice meal."

"Oh, that's really not—"

"Hang on, Avery. Oh, that's perfect, Bert. Josh will take you to that new little Italian place over in Coxsackie."

By the time I hang up, Frieda has extracted my schedule from me, made a reservation, and promised that Josh will pick me up the following evening at seven. She was probably going to offer to take me shopping for a dress to wear if I didn't disconnect when I did.

Telling myself that Josh has had as little control over this scenario as I have, I keep my expectations low even as I spend a ridiculous amount of time getting ready the next evening. Applying the makeup Van gave me in a way that makes me look sexy without looking like I made an extra effort takes time, after all.

Choosing an outfit that says, *I'm just wearing this because it's a nice restaurant, not because I want to seduce you,* is even more of a challenge. Especially after I reject colors not on Van's swatch samples.

It's tough to read Josh's expression when he shows up at my door at exactly seven o'clock, but he's clearly caught unawares when my mother sidles up next to me to ask, "Who's this?"

"Josh Harmon, meet my mother, Patricia Mills."

"Nice to meet you, Mrs. Mills."

As they shake hands, my mother says, "You didn't tell me you were going to dinner with a young man, Avery."

A high-pitched giggle bursts out of me. "Josh isn't a young man, Mom. He's a dad in Playgroup."

When my mother raises a single brow, her expression is *very* easy to read: *Then why are you going on a date with him?*

"And he's doing some work at the rec center too," I add.

A second brow joins the first. "Really? What sort of work?"

"I work for Trede, ma'am," Josh says. "We are funding some changes at the center and I'm working with the staff to facilitate. But I'm taking Avery out tonight as a thank you for stepping in to take care of my kids the other night when my mother had an accident."

Luckily, this snags my mother's interest. After Josh reassures us both that his mother is expected to recover fully, I say, "We'd better get going if we're going to make that reservation."

"Nice to meet you, Mrs. Mills," Josh calls as he guides me toward his car, catching my elbow when I stumble on the uneven sidewalk in front of my parents' house.

"Okay there?" he asks.

"I think you'd know by now that this is par for the course for me," I say, my voice all high and breathy again in response to his touch. "I suppose this sidewalk could use a few repairs."

He gazes up at the beautiful old tree in our front yard. "Unfortunately, this tree's roots are likely causing the damage."

"We're not chopping down a tree to save the sidewalk!"

He winces as he opens the car door for me. "It can be a tough choice. Especially if the tree is old enough that it's in danger of falling."

As he crosses around to the driver's side, I'm reminded of the topic we continue to avoid: what's on the chopping block at Climax Parks and Rec. I need to make my priorities clear so he won't ruin my job, but I don't want to ruin a date with a man I can't seem to stop fantasizing about. If it even is a date. His mother set it up, but he did say he wanted more.

More what, I wonder?

On the way to the restaurant, I try to keep my nerves at bay with small talk about food, from the fact that the restaurant makes its own pasta and sources its ingredients locally to the hugely popular new reality show, *Yes, Chef!* By the time we're seated at a two-top in the candlelit dining room, my stomach's rumbling but my heart continues to skitter from one worry to the next.

Until the waitress shows up with a bottle of wine and a big smile on her face. "I hear we have a special occasion tonight."

"We do?" Josh asks.

Unable to resist the impulse, I grasp his hand and make *Let's play along and see what it gets us* eyes at him. "Oh, honey. Of course we do."

"Well," Josh says, a ghost of a smile lifting the corner of his mouth. "I don't know if I'd call a third anniversary special."

"Whoever made this reservation thinks you deserve to be spoiled, I'd say. They ordered the chef's tasting menu." She begins the uncorking process. "Which includes this very nice bottle of wine."

"A whole bottle?" I wince. "We have to get back to Climax tonight."

Her eyes go wide. "Uh..."

I slap my hands to my face and Josh laughs before clarifying. "To the *town* of Climax."

"Ohhh," the waitress says, her face red. "Sorry, I always forget about that place."

Josh's smile grows, but it's all for me.

"Anyhoo," the waitress says. "Don't worry. If you don't finish the wine, we can recork it and you can take it with you to finish your, uh... celebration at home. In Climax. I'll stop talking about that now."

After explaining the vintage using a bunch of fancy wine words, she pours a tiny bit and offers it to me to taste. I try to get Josh to do it, but he insists, so I do my best. "Tastes like wine!"

"That's good." The waitress grins as she fills our glasses. "As long as there are no food allergies or aversions, we will proceed with the tasting menu."

I rub my hands together. "Sounds amazing."

Once we're alone again, Josh leans across the table to whisper, "I'm sorry. My mother can get a little carried away."

"I'm excited. I've never had a tasting menu. I'm not even sure what one is, exactly. And who knows, if they think we're celebrating, we might get some free stuff."

I'm doing my best to play it cool, but I'm not only worried about work stuff. Fancy restaurants make me nervous, which makes me even klutzier than usual. I inevitably knock over a glass or trip on my way to the bathroom or bump into a waiter carrying a tray full of steaming hot food that ends up in someone else's lap.

That only happened once, thank goodness, but Peter never let me forget it.

This place isn't intimidating, though. It's probably expensive, but it's also homey. There are only three people working the place, and just ten tables. The food turns out to be deceivingly simple. The green salad has the usual cucumbers and tomatoes, but pickled onions and a charred onion-feta dressing make it so tasty that I'm fighting Josh for the last forkful. When the pasta course arrives—cacio e pepe—I almost tell him he can have it all, because my bum doesn't need any more padding.

"Cacio e pepe is a traditional dish from the Lazio region," the server explains. "The phrase means 'cheese and pepper' and that's precisely what it is. Our fresh pasta is tossed with locally made butter along with imported Parmesan and Pecorino. Buon appetito."

Josh won't take a forkful until I do, however, so I twirl a few strands onto my fork and push the plate toward him before putting it in my mouth. But when my tongue wraps around the unexpected explosion of flavor and velvety texture, I can't contain a moan of pleasure.

Blinking my eyes open, I find him staring at me, his expression wolfish. "Still want me to eat it all?"

I grab the edge of the plate and pull it back toward me. "Who gives a flying fish about calories."

We don't quite end up nose to nose with the last strand of pasta ala *Lady and the Tramp*, but it's close.

The rest of the evening goes by in a flash. Everything's so easy between us that I almost forget about all the complications, from the sticky situation at the rec center to the fact that he's a grieving widower. But on the drive home, he goes quiet, and it's not one of those comfortable silences. I'm bouncing back and forth between the impulse to let him off the hook versus the very real desire to kiss him again, when he clears his throat. "I'm sorry, Avery."

"What for?"

"I don't know about you, but this all feels like a setup." When he glances over, confusion must be written all over my face because he adds, "I don't think she broke her ankle on purpose, but everything that followed... my mom's matchmaking came on pretty strong."

"What if I didn't mind?"

He shoots me a skeptical look. "You don't mind being dropped into the middle of my chaos like an unprepared understudy?"

"The last thing I'd want to do is try and replace your wife. Your children's mother." My face heating, my heart pounding, I press on. "But I can't deny that I'd really like to kiss you again."

His gaze doesn't waver from the road ahead, but his fingers grip the steering wheel so tightly that I can see his biceps bunch inside the sweater that stretches across his broad chest.

"But if it's too much too soon, I totally get it," I blurt when he doesn't say anything else.

"It's not that." In the dim interior light of the car, I can just see his mouth twist to the side. "It's just that it was so easy to pretend with you tonight. I felt—feel—more connected to you after knowing you for just a few weeks than I ever did with Lisa. And that seems really fucked up."

"Oh."

He glances over with a wince. "Not what you were expecting to hear, I bet."

My mouth twist mirrors his from a moment ago. "Do you... want to talk about it?"

"It's so complicated." He lets out a long, heavy sigh. "But long story short, Lisa and I were never in love. We got pregnant by accident and decided to try and make it work."

Pregnant twice *by accident?* is the first thing that pops into my mind, but that's where I keep it, because he's right, it does sound complicated.

"She was a brilliant woman," he continues. "And kind. But she had mental health challenges that I didn't learn about until postpartum depression exacerbated them."

My hand flies to my mouth, hoping she didn't end her own life.

"Her death was an accident," he says, either hearing my gasp or reading my mind. "According to witnesses, she was reading on her cell phone and just stepped in front of a city bus."

"Still, that must have been awful."

"She died instantly, so she didn't suffer."

"But for the rest of you?"

"For those of us left behind, yes, it hasn't been easy. Percy was only months old, so he doesn't remember her, but Mabel..." He drifts off but before I can think of anything comforting or understanding to say, he adds, "She lost her mom to depression and then lost her all over again to that fucking bus."

We're quiet for the last few minutes of the drive. Even after Josh pulls up in front of my parents' house and turns off the engine, neither of us speaks.

"Maybe we should—"

I break off when I realize he's saying, "I'd still like to—"

He stops mid-sentence. "Sorry, what were you saying?"

I turn to face him, feeling warm all over. "I'm torn. I feel a connection with you too, but…"

"I have a lot of baggage," he finishes for me.

My own baggage wraps my gut in a viselike grip, the lovely meal we shared now like a boulder in my stomach. "Yeah, well, join the club."

He turns to face me, but before he can ask anything else, I blurt, "What if we just see where this goes? If you're worried about the kids, we can keep it on the down low. No one has to know but us."

He tips his head to the side. "Are you sure you're okay with that?"

My gaze falls to his lips, and my history floats to the box in the back of my brain where I usually stuff it. "I just really want to kiss you again."

"That's funny," he says softly, his arm snaking along my shoulder. "I've been thinking the same thing."

I'm not sure who moves first, but when we meet in the middle, I'm instantly intoxicated. Like I drank the whole bottle of that wine instead of one glass. As he teases along the seam of my lips and grasps the back of my skull, I scrape fingernails along his scalp. When I open my mouth to let him in, I'm swimming in sensation, inside and out, needing to get closer, feel more of him.

When we break for air, panting as our foreheads rest against each other, he chuckles.

Realizing I've crawled halfway across the console, I begin to retreat, but he doesn't let me go. "I'm just laughing because I feel like a horny teenager all over again.

Fogging up windows while I make out with a girl in front of her parents' house. Hoping her dad doesn't show up with a flashlight."

"Or a shotgun?"

He snorts out a laugh. "Exactly."

Tracing a fingertip along his firm jaw, I say, "I guess we'll just have to get creative."

"Or we could just take advantage of being adults with credit cards and camp out in a hotel room."

"As long as it's not one of those *rent a room by the hour* places," I say with a grin. "I'm in."

"Are you kidding me?" he scoffs. "By the time we racked up the hours in one of those places, we may as well have rented a room at the Ritz."

It's my turn to snort out a laugh. "Okay?"

He shakes his head. "Sorry, I've definitely lost my game. What I meant to say is, I'd love to spend a weekend away with you." Cupping the side of my face with his warm palm, he whispers, "Because I want to get to know every inch of you."

chapter
twelve

JOSH

On paper, it's a great idea to plan a weekend away with Avery. Just thinking about it has me hopeful about the future, in a way that I haven't for a long time.

But when we look at our calendars, reality sets in. Mabel starts first grade this week. My parents have plans for two weekends in the upcoming month. They've put off retirement travel to help with the kids, so I can hardly begrudge them time for leaf peeping or a friends' sixtieth birthday party. Meanwhile, Avery's parents need help round the clock, so she has to convince one of her siblings to visit if we're to get away.

In the meantime, I have so much work to do. At this point, I've met with almost every department head at Climax Parks and Rec. Avery and I haven't talked specifically about children's programming, but that's on me. Even after only a few weeks of class, I'm convinced Playgroup is worth keeping around. I'm not ready to make any promises until I can Tetris my way through a full budget, but when I do, at least I know where to find Avery.

It's not at all easy to pin down Travis, on the other hand. He never seems to be in his office. Instead, he's always at a field or basketball court or workout room. And none of these facilities are anywhere near each other. Conrad explained that the Parks and Rec department has picked up abandoned properties over the years to kluge together its facilities, from an old middle school to farmland to a few lots that I'm worried might be brownfield sites. When I finally catch up with Travis, it's late afternoon on a Thursday and he's calling a kids' soccer match.

And by calling, I mean the man is single handedly doing color and play-by-play commentary of a seven-year-olds' game on a Frankensteined sound system at the edge of a field set at a thirty-degree angle.

"Miles Vanderhoost steals the ball for the Hudson Realty Closers, dribbling along the downhill side. He's got impressive footwork but—look at that! His drive is stalled by Jose Rodriguez, defensive back for the Jones Auto Parts' Flash. Nice pass, Jose! Ron Regis kicks the ball to the uphill side where striker Timmy Ballenger scoops it up."

His patter only pauses when the crowd cheers or groans. The guy must know the name of every single kid on both teams, and his enthusiasm for the match is infectious. The parents aren't side coaching or behaving badly. Nor are they staring at their phones. Everyone just seems to be into the game.

When it wraps up, I hover nearby while Travis chats with coaches and players and random other townsfolk, tirelessly and cheerfully fielding an endless stream of questions and suggestions. Twenty minutes later, I get my turn.

"Travis? I'm Josh Harmon from Trede."

Travis slaps his forehead. "Gah. I know I'm supposed to call you back, man. I swear I'm not avoiding you."

I gesture at the cars exiting the parking lot, or parking field, rather. "You've obviously got your hands full."

His smile is wide, like he couldn't be happier about it. "Yeah, I mean, we've got a solid sports program here. Leia said you want to hear about proposed changes, but honestly, I think we're all good."

"What about your facilities? They seem pretty spread out."

"True." He gestures at the folding table on the side of the field, holding sound equipment and what look like spiral notebooks. "Can we talk while I load up? 'Sposed to rain tonight, so I need to pack up."

I look around, wondering why no one's helping him. "Um, sure."

I have to ask a few times before he lets me help him stow equipment in a nearby shed. Travis could probably use some guidance on delegating and making use of volunteers, but instead of making those suggestions, I ask, "How in the heck do you remember all those kids' names?"

He pauses in the act of looping a very long extension cord. "I dunno. Leia calls me a gossip, but I don't see the deets like that. They're the threads holding this community together. I mean, lots of things don't stick in my brain. I don't know the difference between a stock and a bond, I couldn't tell you any state capitals outside of New York's or the difference between the Greek and Roman gods. That stuff's not important to me, though. I care about my kids and this town. The people I can make a difference to. I can't do anything about the rest of the world, so I don't bother to hang on to it."

Curious, I point at my chest, brows up. "What about newcomers like me?"

"We've had a slew of new folks move to town this past year, so I am a bit behind." He scratches his chin. "Let's see. Josh Harmon. Single dad of Mabel and Percy. Your parents moved here to help you out when you got the job at Trede at the beginning of the summer."

My jaw drops. "How the hell do you know all that?"

He holds up a hand. "Don't worry, I do my best to use my powers for good, not evil."

"But how?"

"I've met your mom."

"You have?"

"Yeah. She's a regular in one of my weight training classes. Those ladies like to chat. I just listen. That shit gets stored away in the little folders of my brain like squirrels storing acorns for winter." He shrugs. "I don't do it on purpose. It just happens."

As we finish loading up the shed, we discuss potential improvements, starting with finding him a flatter soccer field. But as we head back to our cars, I have to ask, "Any advice for a fellow single dad?"

He looks over at me. "What's the sitch with the kids' mom? You share custody?"

"She's not, um... she's deceased."

His face falls, and he reaches out to squeeze my shoulder briefly. "Sorry for your loss, man. That I didn't know."

"But now you do," I point out.

He nods solemnly. "I promise not to abuse the privilege."

"So... advice?"

He continues to nod, and his gait slows, like he's considering his words. "Leia and I share custody fifty-fifty, and we're friends. So I know we've got each other's backs when it comes to the kids. Now, we're not always on the same page about everything, so that does add a wrinkle every once in a while."

He stops to face me, hands on hips. "My best piece of advice? Don't hold the reins too tight. Let other people help. That 'it takes a village' thing? It's for real. And we've got a pretty nice village here."

"I guess you would know."

"Damn straight I would."

With the current incubator class ramping things up at Trede for the month of September, everyone except my small team is focused on shepherding the CEOs-to-be through the workshops and coaching sessions designed to prepare them for pitch sessions with venture capital groups at the end of their term. Meanwhile, I've got my own projects to attend to. I've never had anything to do with site restoration, so it's been a steep learning curve overseeing the final changes to the Trede campus. Nurturing contacts in the business community takes time, but attending events like Rotary breakfasts and the Art Co-op's monthly Open Gallery night, makes me feel like I belong here.

It's the Parks and Rec re-org that's keeping me up at

night. It's not just the fact that I want to find room in the budget to keep Playgroup around. There are just so many moving parts, from figuring out how to plan a renovation that won't interfere with class schedules to getting Wanda new accounting software and then getting it installed. The latter isn't part of my job description, but I quickly learned that when Wanda wants something, she gets it.

Which is why I'm in her office at the end of the workday instead of my own.

"I don't know what it is, Wanda, but there's something different about you today," Travis says from the office manager's doorway. Looking over my shoulder, I realize that it's nearly dark.

"Wanda had to pick up her grandkids, so I said I'd wait around until this new program loaded." The computer dings and I click around to make sure everything looks okay. "Which it looks like it finally has. Good thing, because I need to pick up my kids. My parents have a date night planned."

"I know," Travis says. "Frieda told us about it this morning. You and your kids want to come for dinner tonight? It's just crockpot spaghetti and meatballs."

"With your kids? Aren't they, like, teenagers?"

Travis shrugs. "They're fourteen, so they might ignore your little ones, but they don't bite. We do have a dog, though."

"Mabel would love that."

"So come on, then. I'm heading over there now."

Another good thing about small towns: it only takes ten minutes to get anywhere. Even after swinging by Sweet Rewards bakery to grab a box of cupcakes, I make it home in time to corral Mabel and Percy into my car before my parents have to leave. Both kids are very excited to meet two teenagers and their dog, and thankfully, the Blake teens are kind enough to play Go Fish with the little ones while Travis and I get dinner on the table.

We've just settled down to eat when the front door opens. "Hey, Travis, it's me, I'm just—oh, hi, guys!"

Avery takes in the six of us crowded around the table, looking as delighted as she is confused to see us all together.

"Do you live here too, Miss Avery?" Mabel asks.

"No, honey, I'm just here to get Leia's glasses for her because—oop!"

Avery ducks, dodging a meatball flying from Percy's fork. I jump up to retrieve it, but the dog beats me to it, and I end up catching Avery instead.

"Almost landed on my patootie there!" Avery's cheeks go red as she steps out of my arms, like she's been caught doing something naughty. "What's going on? Dads' night?"

Travis shoots me an inscrutable look before raising his glass. "Exactly. Single fathers unite!"

"Zero aura points for that, Dad," Riley says, looking like she's just managing to hold back an eye roll.

"C'mon, girl," Avery says. "Your dad is cool."

"Yeah, I got rizz." Travis splays a hand across his chest, looking wounded.

Riley drops her head into her hands. "Dad. So cheugy right now."

Owen pats his father on the arm. "It's okay, though. We still love you."

"You and Leia want some dinner?" Travis asks. "We've got plenty."

"Thanks, but we're heading to a movie in Coxsackie.

She's buying tickets on her phone right now because my batteries died, which is why I ran in," Avery says, glancing over her shoulder. "I should probably skedaddle. Have fun!"

The rest of the meal passes without interruption, if you don't count Percy feeding half his dinner to the dog. I know my little guy will be crashing soon, but I don't want to leave without helping to clean up, so we settle the kids in front of the TV for one quick show, Mabel snuggled with the dog, Percy curled up next to Owen, and Riley pretending to be bored.

Travis deals with the leftovers while I load the dishwasher, and I almost don't hear his question over the sound of the running water.

"You know that Avery deserves the best, right?"

Turning to face him, I'm surprised at the set of his jaw. Every other interaction I've had with the guy, he's been as easygoing and lighthearted as the family's golden retriever. But he's all bulldog now.

"I, uh... yeah, I do," is all I seem to be able to come up with.

He waits until the counters are clean and the water turned off, but he's still in bulldog mode when he speaks again. "You seem like a decent guy. But Avery hasn't been the same since she came home from Atlanta. I don't know what happened down there, but it probably had something to do with that turd she was seeing, Peter."

I should probably feel insulted that everyone assumes I'm going to screw things up with Avery, but they're probably right. And it's pretty amazing to know that so many people are looking out for her.

"Things are complicated with us, because of changes

I'm making at CPR and my family situation. But I care about her. And I'll do my best to…" To what? Not fuck things up? With my track record, how likely is that? It's selfish, but I can't seem to let her go. "She just fits with us, you know?"

His nod is slow and punctuated with a shrug. "Yeah. I know."

chapter
thirteen

AVERY

I haven't been with a guy for three years. Not since the epic breakup with Peter and everything that came afterward. I know other women have dry spells, but their biggest worries when they find someone they might actually want to get naked with probably have to do with grooming. Making sure all the parts are shaved or waxed or whatever.

Some girls might be proactive and get an STD test, but I'm pretty sure most girls don't have to worry about being a silent carrier of an asymptomatic disease. Germs just lying in wait to wreak havoc on her life all over again.

Like Lisa and Josh, Peter and I got pregnant by accident. Unlike Lisa and Josh, however, Peter and I had been dating for years. But instead of giving birth and suffering from postpartum depression, I almost died and woke up in the hospital with no baby, no fallopian tubes, and my boyfriend calling me a slut.

Turns out, all this—he'd shouted, gesturing at the tubes

and machines keeping me alive—*was caused by an untreated STD. And I sure haven't slept around, so it must've been you.*

Those were the last words he said *to* me, but not the last words he said *about* me. Before I was even discharged from the hospital, he managed to convince all of our mutual friends that I was a lying liar who cheated on him. He called my sister and demanded that she drive down to Atlanta to pick me up. I spent weeks huddled in her guest room, refusing to talk to anyone, until I was well enough to fly back to Atlanta, pick up my car and the boxes of belongings Peter packed up, and drive home to Climax, where I never told anyone exactly what happened.

But now, if I want to explore this attraction to Josh, I have to suck it up and make sure it doesn't happen all over again. Minus the accidental pregnancy, since I can't ever conceive naturally again.

There's a new OBGYN clinic in town with a female doctor, so I'm hoping I won't be completely sex-shamed the way I was three years ago. I'm still nervous as I fill out the patient history, and I can't keep from fidgeting once I'm sitting on the exam table half naked.

At least the room is warm, and the gown is actually made of fabric instead of paper. I'll be sure to mention both in my Yelp review. Unfortunately, when the PA comes in, she goes through my entire history like I hadn't just filled out the form. It's a good thing she took my blood pressure before the inquisition; otherwise, it'd be off the charts.

"Hmm." A little wrinkle appears in her brow.

"Is something wrong?"

"Um. I don't know. I'll just flag this for the doctor."

"You can't tell me?"

She looks up. "I don't mean to worry you. It's really just an inconsistency in your history. I'm sure the doctor can clear it up."

She exits pretty quickly after that, but by the time the door opens again, I feel like my heart could win a horse race. "The PA said that something's wrong," I blurt out.

The petite woman in a trim white coat holds out a hand to me. "I'm Dr. Bautista. Good to meet you, Ms. Mills."

Her smile is as warm as her handshake, which helps to settle me a little. Until she settles on a stool and rolls over to the computer screen, where the same wrinkle appears in her smooth brow, and she makes the exact same "hmm" sound as the PA.

"What's the matter?" It's a good thing this gown isn't paper, or I'd have shredded it by now.

She blows out a breath. "I'm just trying to sort out this salpingitis diagnosis."

"The PID?" I learned way more than anyone ever should about pelvic inflammatory diseases like salpingitis after waking up in the hospital.

She nods, eyes still on the computer. "It says here that you had a salpingectomy after your fallopian tube ruptured due to an ectopic pregnancy."

"That's right." My voice is so thready I'm not sure she heard me, but she continues anyway.

"I'm so sorry for your loss," she says, meeting my eyes with what looks like real compassion before looking back at the screen. "What I'm confused about is the fact that the doctor determined that an STD was the cause of the salpingitis, when there's no record of any test."

"It all happened kind of backward, I guess, because of

the emergency surgery." I have to swallow past the lump of shame blocking my throat. "I didn't know I had an STD, just like I didn't know I was pregnant and didn't know I had the PID, because I didn't have any symptoms until I started bleeding."

"It can be difficult to talk about these things." The doctor hands me a box of tissues, her voice as full of sympathy as her eyes.

I nod, determined to get back on track and get through this. "But after the surgery, the doctor said that the ectopic pregnancy was a result of scarring in the fallopian tubes, due to me having an STD."

The doctor's lips flatten. "But they didn't test for it?"

I shake my head.

"Were you having unprotected sex at the time?"

As I nod, an ugly wave of self-disgust washes over me. "My boyfriend and I weren't using condoms because we'd been together for a while, and I was on the pill. But I guess I didn't take them regularly enough because I got pregnant anyway. So I figured that maybe I'm just bad at birth control."

Peter's harsh words echo in my ears, and it takes everything I've got to keep from pulling the gown over my head to hide. He swore he hadn't cheated, so all I could think was that I'd somehow contracted something before we got together. My freshman year of college, I had a lot of sex. I'd been a bit of a late bloomer, and the attention from so many guys was intoxicating. I always used condoms, but all I could think was that some random guy must have had some random disease that I got anyway. That was the only explanation I could come up with, but Peter didn't believe it. He was sure I was cheating on him.

Dr. Bautista waits patiently while I blow my nose and wipe away the tears chilling my cheeks. Before I can ask her about tests for sneaky STDs, however, she says, "I'm sorry if this is upsetting to you. I don't mean to rehash old trauma. But I have one more question. Did you tell the doctor about your appendectomy?"

"Um, no? What does that have to do with it? That happened, like, years before."

She winces. "Since the ectopic pregnancy was an emergent situation, he might have performed the surgery without checking old records. But he should have asked afterward."

"Why?"

She meets my gaze. "Because it's entirely possible—if you never had symptoms of a sexually transmitted disease—that the PID and subsequent scarring were caused by the appendicitis."

I'm sitting in front of my computer, trying to remember what it is I needed to get done this afternoon, when a throat clearing startles me back to the present moment.

Two throats clearing, I guess, because when I look up, Daisy and Leia fill the doorway to my office.

"Did you..." It takes me a moment to find words. "Um... need something?"

"Just for you to get your head out of your ass," Leia says.

Daisy swats our boss before adding, "We're worried about you. You've been staring at that computer without moving all afternoon."

I didn't cry when the doctor explained how the misdiagnosis might have happened. I didn't cry when she explained that because the doctor removed both fallopian tubes, it's true that I can't get pregnant without IVF treatments, even though I still get periods. I didn't cry on the way back to CPR, even as the losses tallied up, all because a doctor made assumptions about my sex life. But now, looking at my two friends' concerned faces, a sob bursts out of me.

Before I know it, my office door is closed, Daisy's got an arm wrapped around my shoulders and Leia's asking what's wrong.

"I can't," I manage between sobs, "talk about it here."

Leia pulls out her phone and punches buttons, while Daisy rubs my back, murmurs something vaguely soothing, and hands me one tissue after another.

"Travis will take the twins this evening." Leia tucks her phone in her back pocket. "They'll swing by and bring your parents dinner," she says to me before pointing at Daisy. "Then they'll feed your dog."

Leia crosses her arms and nods her head sharply. "We're going to Come Again."

The name of Climax's townie bar is endlessly hilarious to horny teenagers. But to a full-fledged adult—especially one who hasn't had sex in over three years—it's just annoying. Come Again does have a few things going for it, however: excellent draft beer and cider, low prices, and a back patio for when you don't want to deal with the pool-and-darts-playing, small-town-gossiping crowd indoors.

My friends offer to buy me a drink while I stake out seating. I score the firepit with the most stable Adirondack chairs and light the kindling as I try to decide how much of my embarrassing past to share with my friends.

I've carried around the shame of my breakup with Peter like the weighted backpack the teacher doled out for the health class unit meant to show young teens how much of a pain in the tuchus it is to have to take care of a baby. But as I go over everything I learned in this afternoon's appointment, I realize I have nothing to be ashamed of, unless I count the fact that I believed everything the doctor said and let Peter gaslight me into thinking it was all my fault.

How could I not have asked more questions? Gotten a second opinion? Or at least consulted Dr. Google?

Anger begins to devour all that useless shame. By the time the flames flickering in front of me have burned through the twigs and started on the logs, I'm flat out mad. Problem is, I'm as mad at myself as I am at the doctor. I'm also mad at all the people who can have kids but don't want them. I'm even mad at the fucking sheep and cows in all those farms surrounding Climax, with their adorable lambs and baby cows.

Oh shit. I said the f-word in my head.

"Did you just swear?" Daisy asks.

My friends stare at me from the other side of the fire. "Um. Maybe?"

"Start from the beginning," Leia says, handing me a frosty glass of Afternoon Delight, a Peak Finish Cidery favorite. "If you talk it out, you'll at least feel better."

I take a sip of the crisp apple cider to give myself a moment to settle, focusing on its blend of sweet and acid on my tongue. Come Again may be a bit of a dive, but they support all the local breweries and cideries.

Daisy clinks my glass with hers. "Whatever it is, we've got you."

I take in her kind eyes, and then Leia's, which only show concern. We work alongside each other every day, we've known each other forever, but I'm beginning to wonder if, like me, my closest friends keep some things to themselves. Maybe I'm not the only one with shadows in my past. Maybe sharing my ugly story will make it easier for them to trust me with theirs. So I set down my glass and clear my throat.

"I'm going to skip the gory details. Long story short, three years ago I was on an evening shift at the hotel down in Atlanta, and I suddenly felt really bad. Like I had a stomach flu. But when I went to the bathroom and got up from the toilet, there was blood in the bowl. Like, a lot of blood."

Daisy gasps. "Oh my god."

"It was pretty scary." I take a breath, doing my best to stay calm, even though just thinking about it has the fear gripping my gut. "Peter was out with friends, so a co-worker took me to the emergency room. I don't remember the exact sequence of things after that, but I was basically rushed into surgery."

Leia—the most undemonstrative person I know—takes my hand and squeezes it, which gives me exactly what I need to finish.

"When I woke up, I was told that I'd had an ectopic pregnancy and that it had ruptured."

My friends are silent, but when I take in their faces, there's no judgment. Only concern.

"That must have been awful," Leia says softly.

"Did you know you were pregnant?" Daisy asks.

I shake my head. "Nope. I was on the pill."

After a few beats, Leia asks, "So what was the surgery for?"

"Turns out the ectopic pregnancy was just one of the problems. According to the *doctor*," I spit out the word, wondering if anything that shirt-for-brains man said or did was right, "the embryo was stuck in the fallopian tube due to severe scarring caused by pelvic inflammatory disease."

I close my eyes, reminding myself that the next part wasn't true. "Which he also said was caused by an untreated STD."

Both of my friends sit back, like I might still be infected.

"Did you get it from Peter?" Leia asks.

I shake my head again. "Peter immediately jumped to the conclusion that I'd cheated on him."

"What?" Daisy practically yells. "Did you give him the what for?"

I blow out a bitter laugh. "Have you ever been driving along, obeying all the traffic laws, when you notice a cop behind you? And suddenly, you're so afraid that you were doing something wrong that you end up driving erratically?"

Both my friends nod.

"I knew I hadn't been with anyone while I was with Peter, and I knew I'd used a condom with every partner prior to him, but there was the doctor telling me I'd had an STD; there was Peter telling me he didn't give it to me, and I thought I must've gotten it in college or something. That I was careless one time and I'd been carrying this little bomb around, destroying my reproductive system and threatening Peter's health."

Daisy takes my other hand. "That must've been awful."

All three of us stare at the fire for a few moments, my friends flanking me, and I realize that even without the full truth, they're not judging me. They're on my side.

Then Leia shifts, turning toward me. "Wait. Then what happened today?"

I blow out a breath and then gently ease my hand free to take a long sip of cider. "I went to the doctor. To that new clinic?"

Once I catch their nods, I return my gaze to the fire, still finding it difficult to believe how my story has changed. "She told me that it's entirely possible, even probable, that the infection that caused the scarring could've started when my appendix burst in college. The doctor who removed my fallopian tubes never asked about appendicitis, but I guess he should have. And he didn't even do an STD test. He just looked at me, saw a young, unmarried, sexually active woman, and assumed that was the cause."

"Well, that sucks," Leia says, still holding tight to my hand.

"It does. Especially because I thought I'd be with Peter forever."

"But he didn't believe you!" Daisy cries. "Fuck that guy."

I lift my glass in salute. "Yeah. Fuck that guy."

Typically, when Daisy whips out her tarot deck or bag of runes, I inwardly roll my eyes and just pretend to play along. I may not believe in her woo-woo, but it means a lot to her. But after my big confession, she insists that we throw our old fears into the fire.

Literally.

She pulls a notebook out of the boho monstrosity I call her bag of tricks, shoves pens and paper at us, and tells us to write down our greatest regrets. It doesn't take me long. After all, I just dredged up my sordid past for them. So I write, *believing the doctor and Peter*. And then after a few moments, I add, *not trusting myself*.

After I fold up my paper, I look to Daisy for further instruction. While she finishes whatever she's doing with her own—eyes closed, mumbling something while fervently pressing it against her sternum—I steal a glance at Leia. What I see on her face makes my heart skip a beat.

My boss-friend keeps her emotions close to the vest. She always did, but when she got pregnant at seventeen, she locked it all down and just powered through. From finishing her senior year while breastfeeding twins to working her way up CPR's ranks while taking night classes at the community college, I've never seen her flinch away from a challenge.

But right now, her piece of paper balled up in her fist, I swear she's regretting something big time. Before I can find the guts to ask her about it, Daisy's bright green eyes pop open, and she flings her paper into the fire with a whoop, ordering us to follow suit.

It actually feels good to pitch my old fears at the flames. To watch as the edges curl and blacken, swallowing my words as the paper collapses on itself. When there's nothing left but smoke, it's almost like there's new space in me. One space in particular that would like to be filled to the hilt over and over again in a thrusting fashion.

But also in my heart.

For the past couple years, I've been telling myself that I'm fine. Happy, even. Happy to fill in for my mom with the toddlers, happy to be the problem solver and the shoulder to cry on, happy I can be here for my parents. But what happens when they're gone?

And I'm left alone?

If I'm not the giant fudge up I thought I was, maybe I deserve a person—a family—of my own. A ready-made one with a space for a mom.

Slow down, girl. You've barely kissed the guy and you hardly know him.

What you do know: he's likely planning to cut the toddler program that's the highlight of your week. Even if he and his son love it, he may not have a choice.

Plus, he might not be married, but he's grieving.

Though I think I read somewhere that sex can be healing. If only we can find the time.

When I crawl into bed later that night, the buzz from the cider has worn off, but Daisy and Leia's love is still wrapped around me like a cozy blanket. Whatever happens with me and Josh, my friends will have my back.

fourteen

JOSH

Halloween in Manhattan could be fun, with kids running up and down condo hallways and meeting neighbors you barely knew existed, but it was nothing like the holiday I remembered growing up. Even before I was old enough to trick-or-treat without adult supervision, it was exciting to be outside past bedtime. To see the houses transformed by colored lights and spooky decorations, even to be frightened by scary costumes.

I've been determined to give my kids as much of the smalltown Halloween experience as possible, so when I got a newsletter from Bedd Fellows Farm announcing the mid-September kickoff of their pumpkin patch, I figured it'd be a great way to get us all in the mood. Since my dad's out of town for a golf tournament this weekend, I ask my mom if she wants to visit the farm with me and the kids Saturday morning.

But she begs off, pointing to her ankle. "I'll just slow you all down."

My mom's in a boot and pretty mobile around the

house, so I hadn't even thought about the challenges the farm might present. "Do you want us to stick around here? It'll be happening all next month too."

She waves this down. "I've got a good book to read. Just bring me back a treat."

As the kids and I get dressed, I impulsively call Avery and invite her to join us instead.

"Are you sure?" she asks.

The tentativeness in her voice has me pushing harder. "Of course. You think I can keep up with both of these monsters on my own?"

I'm relieved to hear her laugh. "Are you speaking literally? Are Percy and Mabel dressing up as monsters?"

"No costumes required." I drop my voice. "Unless you want to go for the sexy milkmaid, that is."

"I'll see what I can do," she purrs in a tone that heats me to my core, making me worry that I'm playing with fire.

Twenty minutes later, we pull up in front of Avery's house. Before I can get to the door, she steps through it and my mouth goes dry as I take in skintight jeans tucked into boots and the plaid shirt tied at the waist revealing a hint of pale skin. "Forget sexy milkmaid," I mutter. "I'll take sexy cowgirl any day."

The minute we get to the pumpkin patch, Mabel drags Avery to see the star of Bedd Fellows Farm, a sheep called Baabara Streisand. I hear the woolly animal lives in some sort of pet palace up by the house, but at the moment she's posing for photos with fans.

Meanwhile, Percy runs in the other direction. I just manage to catch him before he clambers onto a pile of pumpkins. "Whoa, boy. I think this is a *you break it, you buy it* situation."

"Actually, this is the pumpkin mountain." Sam Bedd appears next to me, clapping a hand on my shoulder. "So many kids wanted to climb on the pumpkins we just made it a thing. Go for it, little man."

Another preschooler joins Percy, and as Sam and I watch them in silence, I remember that my old roommate was always easy to just hang out with.

"Do you ever feel like a fraud?" With anyone else, I'd have to work my way up to this question. But this is how Sam and I talked. We could be working in our room for hours and one of us would throw out a random question. Even now, it doesn't seem weird to bring up something that would be embarrassing with anyone else.

As expected, Sam doesn't question the question. "You mean that thing where you think someone's going to walk in your office and say, 'You have no idea what you're doing. Get out.' That thing?"

"Uh, yeah, I guess. Except it's not just in the office. It's everywhere."

Sam's gaze follows Percy, now trying to move a pumpkin half his size. "Well, nothing prepares you for parenting all by yourself, I'm sure. And you seem to be doing a pretty good job of that."

"Maybe. Better than I did when Lisa was still around, ironically. At least I'm present."

"And she wasn't?"

"Not on purpose. She was... depressed."

"That must have been hard."

"I think it was. She never really let me in."

Sam's dog wanders up, and he squats to scratch behind Gomer's ears. After a long moment of staring into the dog's eyes, he looks up at me. "It wasn't your job to fix her, you know."

"Yeah," I say, even though I still believe I should have been able to.

"Anyway, I meant that it must have been hard on you and the kids."

"It was definitely hard on them. I know they miss her, but they are happier now. Without that... I don't know, weight in the house."

"So what's this feeling like a fraud thing about, then?"

"You know I've never had a job interview? I've had two positions just handed to me. Both times, because of Lisa."

"Are you sure this isn't one of those *You didn't go to a real Ivy League, you just went to Cornell* kind of things? Because that's some dumb bullshit."

Lisa did manage to work our degrees into more than one conversation—that she graduated from Yale while I just attended one of Cornell's state colleges—but that wasn't the real problem.

"In New York," I continue, "her family used their connections to get me my first job so we could be closer to them. Because I got her pregnant."

"Well, there must've been more to it than—"

"And then Eli felt sorry for me and created this job for me at Trede."

Sam shrugs. "Lots of people get hired because of connections. Most people get a leg up one way or another."

"Did you?"

"Uh, no. But my job does require a pretty specific skill set."

"Exactly. I have no skills."

"Did you get fired from your first job? Because you were incompetent?"

"No. I left. My kids needed me."

"So, you must've had some aptitude for what you were doing. Nepotism is real, but unless you're the owner's first-born, you can't let the milk go bad. You've got to churn some butter."

"Is that a new saying I'm unaware of?"

"Nah, I'm just hungry." He slaps his belly. "Anyway, when it comes down to it, all you can do is your best. That's what I'm working on anyway. I don't have to be good at everything or know how to do everything. I just have to know enough to ask the next question. And be humble enough to get help when I need it."

"Where'd you learn this philosophy? Your new girlfriend?"

"Don't tell Diane"—he leans closer and lowers his voice—"but I learned it from my dog."

Before I can ask what he means by that, two little arms grab me from behind. "Daddy! Guess what?"

One eye on Percy, who seems to be getting along with the other kids on the pumpkins, I reach around to sweep Mabel into my arms. "What?"

Avery jogs up and drops her hands to her knees to catch her breath. "Whew! Mabel, you're fast."

Mabel pats me on the chest. "I wanted to tell Daddy about the cows. A mommy cow's baby died, and a baby cow's mommy died so they adopted each other."

A woman who looks vaguely familiar steps up next to Avery. "Wait. Mabel is Josh's daughter?"

"Do you remember my twin sister, Colleen?" Sam asks me. "She visited a couple times freshman year."

"Right!" I set Mabel down so she can join the kids on the pumpkins. "For a writing conference or something?"

"Good memory." Colleen draws a line between me and Avery. "But how do you two know each other?"

Avery tells her about Playgroup and Trede but doesn't say anything else about whatever we are to each other. Which is fair, since we can't seem to get beyond *really like kissing but have a lot of baggage.* When Avery begins to ask about the rest of the Bedd family in detail, I have to ask, "So how do you guys know each other?"

"Well, duh," Colleen says. "We went to the same high school."

Avery, obviously reading my blank look, adds, "Fork Lick is even smaller than Climax, so the county high school serves both, plus a few other hamlets."

"Colleen and Avery started a library club," Sam adds. "So they could get the school to buy romance books."

"And so we could have somewhere quiet to eat lunch," Colleen says, swatting at her brother.

A wistful smile crosses Avery's face. "Luckily, the school board didn't pay too much attention to content back then."

"Ugh." Colleen shudders. "Don't even get me started on the books those idiots want to ban these days."

Avery and Colleen talk about old friends while Sam and I chat about his new job for a bit, but a howl from Percy has me stopping him mid-story. "Sorry, man. I think we need to wrap this up. Naptime's a calling."

"No worries." Sam tips his head toward a table where Diane's ladling out apple cider. "I should probably check in with the boss, anyway. Don't be a stranger."

As we strap two exhausted, sun-kissed children into their car seats, each holding a kid-sized pumpkin, I realize that I don't feel like a stranger. And when I open Avery's door for her, waiting for her to sit before handing her the pastry box full of apple turnovers, I feel something even more precious.

Like I'm with my family, and we're heading home.

chapter
fifteen

I can't control all the forces keeping Josh and me from escaping for a weekend alone, so I may as well focus on the positives from the past week, such as: Theo pooped in the potty for the first time, I got an adorable photo of me and Mabel and an internet famous sheep, and on the way back from the farm, Josh and I finally talked frankly about children's programming at CPR.

The discussion wasn't as horrible as I'd thought it would be, but the statistics are pretty depressing. He says he's doing his best to save Playgroup because he gets its value, but we have to think about what's best for all in Climax, not just a handful of families.

If I weren't so sexually frustrated, I'd be happy right now. Josh and I have snuck in a couple of make out sessions, each of which left me wanting more. They say that's a good thing, but I'm having a hard time finding the good in deprivation. Especially now that I know I'm disease-free and don't even have to worry about birth control.

Which brings up a tricky question. Do I tell Josh that I can't have kids, at least without expensive interventions? What if he wants to have more? He's such a great dad, I'd hate to deprive him of that possibility. Fresh anger at the healthcare system that has left me with a broken womb, my mom with a disease that no one understands, and my dad with pain that doctors can't manage has me groaning so loudly that I almost miss the chime from my phone.

Eager for distraction, I snatch it up.

JOSH

Kids in bed. Wish I was in bed with you

ME

Same, dude.

JOSH

I'm sorry my life is so complicated

ME

You're not alone

JOSH

Are you alone?

ME

Of course!

JOSH

Just wasn't sure if you were in bed
or what

ME

I'm in bed

All alone

The three dots appear and disappear several times. I'm

staring at them, face hot, wondering if that was too much of a hint or if I should say more, when the photo I took of Josh smirking at me over a plate of pasta flashes on the screen. Fumbling to swipe and accept his call, I accidentally hit speaker.

"Hi," I whisper. "Um, you're on speaker."

"I thought you were alone," he says, his voice so low and growly that my deprived Pandora's box clenches, jonesing for a special someone to surround.

"I am," I say, the heat of a blush spreading from my cheeks to my chest. "It's just, I mean, I don't know. I'm in my childhood bedroom. I feel like I'm going to get in trouble for talking to a boy late at night. In fact, I'm going to put in my earbuds. Hang on."

After I do so and tell him that I'm back, he asks, "Did teenage Avery talk to boys late at night?"

I snort. "Only about homework. Teenage Avery was very nerdy. She didn't, um, find herself until college."

"Oh yeah? What did she find?"

"That she liked sex."

"I'd like to hear exactly what she liked. Likes. Can you tell me?"

Without direction, my free hand slides inside my sleep shorts. "Are we having phone sex?"

"Do you want to?"

"I never have, but... yeah, I think so." A nervous giggle pops out of me. "What do we do?"

"I've never tried it either, so don't laugh if I ask a cheesy question."

"Like?"

"What are you wearing?"

"Do you want the truth?"

"Of course."

"Sleep shorts and a tank top."

"Tell me more about them. So I can picture you." His voice has dropped, in pitch and volume. I hear rustling, like he's moving around.

A little shiver goes through me, and my heart drops. Like waaay south. "Well, they're not very fancy. But they're super soft. Black, stretchy, cottony things."

"Are they loose or tight?"

"Um, the top is tight. I like to feel like my boobs are contained, I guess. But the bottoms are pretty loose."

"So if I was there, I'd have a hard time slipping my hand inside the top, but not the bottoms?"

Another shudder rolls down my torso, obliterating all worries about work-life Josh because personal-life Josh is... So. Dang. Hawt. "Yep," I answer, my voice reedy. "That's correct."

"Hmm. Where should we start?"

"I guess that depends."

"On what?"

"Are you a boob man? A butt man? A leg man? Or..."

"I appreciate the entire package, actually. But I think I'd start by exploring the gap between the bottoms and the top."

I'm glad he can't see my grimace. "Ugh."

"That doesn't do it for you?"

"It's just, I don't exactly have a six-pack."

He snorts. "Neither do I. Overrated, if you ask me. Besides, I'm imagining how soft that skin is. How it would feel if I ran my palm over your belly."

"It's soft all right."

"Can you do it? Tell me what you feel? What you see?"

I set the phone on the pillow next to me, push down the covers, and pull up my shirt. As my fingers trace the noticeable scars near my belly button, I realize I might have to tell Josh about the salpingectomy before we get naked in person. Pushing that to the side for the moment, I sit up on my elbows. "Um, my skin's pretty pale. I burn easily, so I avoid the sun as much as possible."

"Which makes it even softer, I bet."

"It is soft. The skin is very soft, and—" Self-consciousness about my pear shape fades as I lie back and imagine Josh exploring my torso. "I can just feel the tiny hairs under my fingers."

"And if you move your hand farther down? What's the hair like?"

I can't help but snort. "Well, the curtains don't exactly match the drapes."

He laughs. "I never knew exactly what that meant, but I think I get the idea. You're saying the carpet isn't honey gold and straight? Or is it the curtains?"

"The ones the world doesn't see are short and curly and light brown."

"And if I ran my fingers through it and dipped in between the curls to your folds, would you be wet right now?"

"I..." My mouth is suddenly dry, like all the moisture inside fled south. "Don't know."

"Will you check for me?"

His voice holds the perfect blend of dare and curiosity, and I'm completely in its thrall as his questions shift to requests and then to commands. My eyes close as the fingers of my right hand circle. As he tells me how hard he is for me, how he's pumping his length, wishing he was inside me, I can almost feel his weight and warmth on top of me. My fingers rub harder, and my hips lift off the bed, demanding more.

His breath is labored as he urges me on. "Yes," he moans. "I want to hear you come, Avery. Will you come for me?"

My answer is lost in gasps and a keening whine as a climax rocks me hard. Aftershocks continue to pulse beneath my hand as he releases a guttural moan followed by a low laugh.

And then I'm laughing too. My hand still tucked between my legs, I curl into a ball to face the phone next to me, giggling.

Several minutes later, we both seem to settle, and I let out a sigh. "Wow."

"Yeah?"

"Now I can't wait to do that IRL."

At this point, I'd settle for just *seeing* Josh IRL. First, he was out of town for work. When he returned, the only times he was free, I either had a CPR event or one of my parents needed me.

Phone sex has been kind of fun, liberating even, but it's getting to the point where my Petunia is aching to be filled with his Richard. I assigned "Bed Chem" as his ringtone, and I'm definitely manifesting every time he calls. Even a text notification from him has me crossing my legs and grabbing my phone like a teenager.

JOSH

Just found out that my parents will be
home the first two full weekends in Oct

ME

I'll check with my sibs

Crossing my fingers, I type a message into the group
chat my brother, sister, and I use to keep in touch. I've
already broached the idea of me needing a break from full-
time parent care, so I'm hoping one of them can step up.

ME

Remember when I talked about trying to
leave town for a weekend? Anybody
available to stay with Mom and Dad 10-5
or 10-12 weekend?

My siblings are busy people, and they say watched pots
don't boil, so I make myself leave my phone in my room
and go down to the kitchen to clear out my parents' email
and pay bills. By the time I'm balancing the checkbook, a
bowl of ice cream is required. But I get it done, and then,
hoping to find a reward, I jog back to my room.

Unbelievably, my brother and sister have had a full-on
conversation in my absence. Turns out my sister Carla and
her wife are available one of the weekends I suggested. My
brother even adds his regrets.

Switching over to the text thread with Josh, I give him
the dates and hope he's still free.

JOSH

Perfect! I'm putting it in the family
calendar *in pen* rn, and I'll book a place
tomorrow.

ME

Can't wait

JOSH

Let me know if you have any requests

ME

For the whoopee making?

JOSH

😂For the hotel

ME

😊I'll shut up now

JOSH

😳

ME

XXOO

night

JOSH

Sweet dreams

If there's one thing I'm sure of, my dreams are not going to be anywhere near as sweet as my words.

chapter
sixteen

JOSH

Just as I walk into my office after another very productive meeting with Carl Conrad at CPR, who is a font of good ideas, my phone rings. Thinking it might be Avery, since I somehow missed her at the rec center, I snatch up the receiver. "Hello?"

"Hello to you too, Josh. So glad to have caught you."

I have to stifle my groan when I recognize Martina Diaz's voice. "Yes, it's been hectic around here. What can I do for you, Mayor?"

"You can attend the public-private partnership conference I told you about."

"I tried," I say, "but registration was closed."

"Lucky for you, I pulled a string or two and got two tickets. One for Trede and one for CPR. The focus is community center development, so it's perfect."

Pulling out my cell, I open my calendar app. I had checked out the conference when she told me about it weeks ago, but when we couldn't get in, I deleted it from my memory cache. "When was that again?"

When she reminds me, I slump into my desk chair. Naturally, the conference is the one weekend Avery and I have planned to leave town. "Which stakeholders did you tell them would attend?"

"Ideally, it'd be you and Leia Blake. Unless there's someone else from either organization involved in the current collaboration."

"And when do you need confirmation?"

"There are grant opportunities specifically targeted to attendees of this conference. It'd be a shame to miss out on them." Before I can figure out a decent excuse for why I can't go, she adds, "Especially since I went to the trouble to get you in."

"Right. I do appreciate it."

"I'll get on the horn with Leia and tell her you'll be there, then," she says.

Just as I'm about to give in, Eli appears in my doorway. "Mayor, give me an hour to figure this out. I'll talk to Leia and get back to you."

"As long as someone shows up."

"I'll confirm with you by the end of the day."

Eli sits down as I'm hanging up. "What's this you have to figure out with the mayor and Leia?"

"I thought we were meeting at four."

Reaching across my desk, he picks up the CPR plan that has my notes written in the margins. The notes I planned to work into the final version before our meeting.

"We were, but I saw you in here, and honestly, it'd be better for me if we meet now. Then I could catch an earlier flight to New York."

"What's happening in New York?"

"Venture capital crap." Eyes on the document in his hands, he asks, "You can do this now, right?"

"Well, I'm not really finished prepari—"

He frowns. "Josh, it's just me."

"Yeah, and you're my boss."

"We're still friends."

I suppress a sigh. He was *friends* with Lisa. Until I moved to Climax, she was always part of the equation. He likely doesn't get that there's a power dynamic between us, either. The same way Lisa never got the difference between parents who paid for every little thing at Yale versus parents who could barely scrape together the money for state school tuition.

I blow out a breath. "Yes, we're friends. But I'd like to make sure the plan is clear, so that—"

"So let's break it down. Pretend I'm not your boss." He jumps up, circling his hands between us. "No bad ideas. Let's whiteboard it."

I press my lips together and count to five before speaking to calm my mind. If I count to ten, he'll keep talking. "We're past that, Eli. We've got plans in place. Plans the mayor has signed off on."

His brow furrows. "Since when?"

"Since Tuesday? When I met with her?"

He looks up and to the left. "When I was in San Francisco?"

I shrug. "Possibly."

"Damn it, Josh. You can't sneak in meetings behind my back."

"Eli. It is my job to shepherd this project. From conceptualization to fruition. You can't be there for every little meeting. You have your own job. You're the CEO, remember? I'm just one of your many VPs."

He rests a hip on the table and flips through the plan, muttering, "But this is more fun."

Speaking the truth, as in, *because it's the latest thing and you'll get bored and move on soon enough,* would not be a wise move. Instead, I shift gears. "Do you not trust me?"

Frowning, he crosses his arms over his chest. "All right. Show me what you've decided."

When the last word lands with complete derision, I tell myself that I knew it'd be like this. Eli has mood swings and if you want the good, you have to accept the asshole every once in a while. This time I do count to ten as I open my laptop and sync it with the smartboard. Then I remind myself why I took this job. So my kids and I could live in a place that was more down to earth than Manhattan.

A slideshow of images flashes through my head, making me realize that it's no longer just a job to me. Reconnecting with Sam, bonding with Travis and the parents at Playgroup, every moment I've spent with Avery... These moments make it clear that I'm part of this town.

"Okay," I begin, clicking through the first slides. "This should all look familiar. Same open design. However, we've decided to shift some of the space usage and some of the programming."

As I go over the plans, I skim quickly past the inclusion of Playgroup, hoping he won't notice the fancy footwork I've done to keep it there. Instead, I focus on the multipurpose room and makerspace, neither of which were in our original plans.

"Multipurpose room? Isn't that what they have now? That horrible combination of stage and basketball court?"

"This would be much more adaptive than the current gymnatorium."

"And where's the Pilates room? The barre studio? The cycling suite?"

"There are already private gyms in Climax. And we have those specialty rooms here at Trede."

"But we have to have places for employees' family members to work out. And appropriate activities to keep their progeny occupied while they do so."

"But the spouses of Trede's employees are a minority of the population."

"So far."

"Do you plan to repopulate the entire county?" Only half kidding, I wonder if that is what he's thinking.

"I need to give the town a makeover if I want to have a chance at attracting the best talent. That's what I brought you here to do."

"You brought me in to connect with the community. It was your idea that I start with the Parks and Rec department. Which serves everyone in the town."

"And it will be open to all of Climax."

"But if it's filled with programs and spaces that aren't welcoming to all, then it'll only serve an elite few."

"What are you saying? I need a damn Walmart greeter at the door?"

Surprised that he even knows such a thing exists, I close the computer and meet Eli's gaze. "Throwing down money to build a shiny new thing will actually cause problems, Eli. Replacing Zumba with Pilates will just alienate people."

"But I'm giving this to the town."

"Gifts that come with strings attached are a double-edged sword. If you don't wield that sword carefully, it'll be destructive. But if you use your money to make people's lives better—"

"Doing CrossFit and barre and Soul cycle classes would fix the diabetes problems, I'd bet."

"Only if people showed up to the classes. We have an opportunity to solve actual problems here, to fill real gaps in the town infrastructure."

"I'm not building a church, Josh."

"It'd be better than a church, because it won't be based on a patriarchal structure. Imagine a center designed to build community. With spaces where people can have fun, learn things, exercise, and meet people outside of their jobs and families and social strata. That's not just a way for Trede to get tax breaks from the local government."

I take one big breath, because if this doesn't land, I'm fucked. "Eli, a place that centers community isn't just a building. It's a legacy."

He just stares at me for so long, I'm not even sure that my words register. But I hang in there, hoping that they'll reach the kind heart I suspect lies deep inside my prickly boss.

"Fine," he finally says. "But if there's no Pilates, I'm not paying for everything."

Sending up thanks to whatever gods are in charge of recreation, I smile. "Funny you should mention that."

I don't know if it's because he's eager to get out of town or what, but Eli signs off on Trede's participation at the public-private partnership retreat without a fight. "You get Leia Blake there, and I'll be there," he says before heading out back to a waiting helicopter.

My high doesn't last long, unfortunately, because Leia Blake does put up a fight.

"Hmm," is all the Parks and Rec director has to say in response to my excellent pitch selling her on the advantages of attending the PPP workshop as a means of garnering additional funding for the CPR redevelopment. "I thought this was your job."

"Community development is my job. But input like this—financial, educational, and institutional—can be invaluable when you're setting a new course. I've gained so much from conferences like these. I really don't think it's an opportunity you want to turn down."

"I still don't get why you aren't going."

Because I want to get out of town for a sex-fest with your best friend?

"Because it can be most advantageous for the top stakeholders to participate. Really get the juices flowing. Shake things up."

"Top stakeholders? So if not you, who would be going from Trede?"

I shut my eyes, trying to figure out if I can stretch the truth enough to get her there without outright lying.

"Elijah's going, isn't he?"

Fuck. I bite back the curse and force a smile. "He's invested in the success of the partnership, after all."

"Well, if he's going, I'm not going."

Double fuck.

"Why don't you sleep on it, and we can talk about it more tomorrow?"

"Sleeping on it will not change my mind. We had a deal. I work with you. Not Eli. You renege on that deal, you lose my support. All of it."

I'm left with the dial tone echoing in my ear and my dick not speaking to me.

chapter
seventeen

AVERY

"Avery? Hello?"

"Yes?" I look up to find Leia standing in my office doorway talking to me. By the look of frustration on her face, she's been there for quite a while.

"You have a funny look on your face." Eyes narrowing, she plops down in the chair across from me.

"Must've been something I ate." I jab the keyboard like I'm actually working here instead of fantasizing about all the ways I'm going to get Josh naked this weekend. "Did you need something?"

She sighs so heavily, I stop pretending to be engrossed in whatever's on my computer screen. "What's the matter?"

She grimaces, like she just ate something terrible. "I need a favor."

"Sure. Anything. You need me to drive the kids somewhere?"

She sighs again. "I need you to go to a conference on public-private partnerships this weekend."

Nooo! "This weekend? As in, like three days from now?"

"Yes," she spits out. "When a person says this weekend, they're typically referring to the one coming up."

Son of a mother trucker. It's like the universe is trying to keep me and Josh apart. "It's such short notice, I—" I can't use my parents as an excuse because my sister is coming. So I can go away and come with Josh.

"It's important."

"Then why aren't you going?"

She rolls her eyes, like she can't believe she's about to say what she's about to say. "Elijah is going."

I just raise my eyebrows.

"And yes, fine. I'm not—I mean, I'm over him. It's not like that. I'm just... still so angry with him. And he irritates the hell out of me, and I don't think I will be at my best." Her hands flail around for a moment. I've never seen Leia look so helpless. "The mayor called. She basically said that this is an opportunity we can't refuse."

When the mayor uses language like that, you can't say no.

She presses her palms together. "Can you please go? I'll do whatever your parents need."

Fudge nuggets.

I can't say no to her puppy dog eyes, so I look at my computer and click around for a moment. Maybe it's a sign. Josh and I just have too much baggage between the two of us. I may not be infected with a silent killer of an STD, but I can't have kids, and he probably wants to be with a woman with a working womb. Maybe I'll learn something at this conference that will help me find a way to save Playgroup or come up with an alternative that will serve more of the population.

"Sure. I'll go. No problem."

ME

Bad news

JOSH

You too?

ME

What's your bad news?

JOSH

You first

ME

No you

JOSH

Okay

The mayor signed up Trede and CPR for a conference this weekend and I tried to send your boss and mine but yours wouldn't go with mine and now mine says he won't go if she's not going

I have to read the sentence a couple times before I realize it could actually be good news.

ME

So who *is* going?

JOSH

I have to go. Which means we can't get away. I'm so sorry.

ME

Funny thing

MY boss is making ME go

JOSH

WHAT

ME

So it looks like we *are* getting a weekend away...

JOSH

I can't believe I didn't think of this

ME

I mean, we will have to work

JOSH

Only some of the time

ME

Hmmm. What will we do with the time in between workshops...

JOSH

Don't worry. I've got ideas.

chapter
eighteen

JOSH

Even though we're going to be on the clock much of the weekend, driving to the retreat center in the Berkshires with Avery feels like skipping school. Especially when she starts reading the list of activities from the retreat center website.

"Zip-lining? Go Karts? Paint by numbers? What is this place?"

"You tell me," I say. "I didn't make the arrangements; the mayor did."

"The mayor."

When I glance over, Avery's expression matches her tone: dread. But then her brow relaxes, and she catches her bottom lip between her teeth. "Is that bad?"

She chuckles. "The mayor is a bit of a matchmaker."

"Are you saying that this whole thing was a setup?"

"Welll..." She raises both palms. "Could be a *two birds with one stone* situation. Maybe she really did want reps at this conference."

"But she's also playing Cupid?" Before she can answer, I add, "But with who?"

"What do you mean?"

I glance over at her. "She thinks Leia and I are going on this trip."

Avery laughs. "I said she was a matchmaker. I didn't say she was a good one."

Whatever the mayor's intentions, I'm thankful for the result. I'd much rather be taking a drive with Avery than with her boss. Or my boss for that matter. It's not just the anticipation of finally getting a chance to get naked with her. Just being with Avery has me buzzing with all kinds of good feelings. Anticipation, hope... eagerness to get on with living my life instead of just existing.

As we're getting back in the car after a pit stop for gas, coffee, and a snack, Avery draws a finger back and forth between us. "We should keep this private at the conference, right?"

I sift through the many possible motivations behind her question before leaning across the console to give her a kiss as full of promise as I can make it. When I sense her relaxing, I pull away just far enough to meet her gaze, keeping a hand on her cheek. "I will do whatever makes you most comfortable."

When her shoulders rise toward her ears, I add, "We don't have to decide right now what to tell people. But in my book, my status isn't 'complicated.' It's 'in a relationship.' With you."

Her cheeks pink up, and she grabs my face with both hands to kiss me again.

"Okay, okay," I murmur when we come up for air. "Unless you want to make another stop at a rent-by-the-hour hotel, let's get there already so we can make the best use of our time."

"Fine," she says, falling back into her seat with an exaggerated groan. "But we need to get naked the minute we check in."

After we cross the Hudson, we take roads curving through the Taconic and Berkshire hills into Massachusetts. When we arrive at the address, however, Avery asks, "Are you sure this is it? The sign says it's a camp."

"The car navigation says so, but it's not always right. Should we check the website again?"

Avery pulls out her phone and taps the link from the confirmation email I'd sent last night. After she scrolls through the site for a few moments, she says, "Ohhh, I see."

"Are we in the right place?"

"Yep. This place used to be a summer camp. They repurposed it." She looks out the window as I continue up the driveway bordered by forest on one side and open fields on the other. "It's kind of perfect. I mean, what better place to learn about recreation?"

After being greeted and directed to parking by smiling young people in what I'd bet are artificially faded Camp Wildwood t-shirts, we head up to the main lodge. We're a bit early for check in, so it's quiet in the lobby until the woman in front of us lets out a groan. "Are ye sure, lad? I've been registered for this conference for months."

The clerk taps away at a keyboard for a moment before shaking his head. "I'm so sorry. We don't have a reservation with that name. Is there a business or organization it might be under?"

As they confer, I turn to Avery and raise my brows. "Should I...?"

She nods, her grin impish. "Works for me."

"Excuse me," I begin, catching the clerk's eye. "Sorry to interrupt, but I couldn't help but overhear."

The woman turns to face me, her expression apologetic. "I just can't believe they don't have a cabin for me. I came all the way from Dublin for this."

"We"—I draw a line in the air between Avery and myself—"have two cabins reserved, but can make do with one."

"There was a last-minute change and we're here in place of our bosses," Avery explains.

"Are ye sure? Ye wouldn't mind sharin'?"

If I weren't already planning to spend every free moment naked with Avery, the older woman's Irish accent would've charmed the room out of me. "It's no problem."

"None at all," Avery echoes.

The woman darts a look between the two of us before smiling broadly and stepping to the side. "Let's see if we can get this sorted, then."

While the clerk and I consult, Avery and the woman introduce themselves. By the time I hand each woman a key, they've made plans to meet up for a drink during the cocktail hour.

"Frances O'Leary," the woman says, shaking my hand. "Least I can do is buy you a pint."

After studying the campus map, we're encouraged to take one of the golf carts to our cabin, since it's located on the other side of the lake.

"Did you ever go to summer camp?" she asks, her tone soft as we drive along the path.

"I did for a few years."

She turns to me, brows up. "Did you have a camp sweetheart?"

"That would be a no. I was like eight, nine, ten years old."

"You didn't have crushes on girls back then?"

"I did. But for one, I went to a boys' camp. And for two, girls scared the bejeezus out of me."

"No sisters, huh? Or too many sisters?" She sits back in her seat. "Wow, I don't even know if you have siblings."

"I know you have one sister, and she is my favorite because she's staying with your parents right now."

"I also have a brother, who now owes me," she says with a contented sigh. "And you?"

"I'm an only. My parents wanted more, I think, but couldn't have them for some reason."

"That's sad."

When I glance over, she's squinting, her eyes likely blinded by the bright reflection of the sun on the lake. "Do you need a hat? I might have an extra in my bag somewhere. Though it's probably kid-sized."

She shakes her head and smiles at me, blinking away moisture from her eyes. "It's fine." Looking down at the map, where the clerk circled our cabin, she peers ahead before pointing to the right. "I think we're down there."

The cabins look rustic from the outside, but after we punch in the code and haul our bags inside, it's obvious they've been upgraded considerably from the days they were chock-full of bunkbeds. "This is nothing like what my camp cabin looked like, by the way."

Dropping her computer bag on a table behind a sofa facing what looks like a working fireplace, Avery heads farther into the space, rolling her suitcase behind her. When I hear her gasp, I rush to catch up.

"Everything okay?"

When I enter the bedroom, she's standing in the middle of it, turning in a slow circle. "I never want to leave this room."

I'm sure it's very nice, but in this moment, I can only take in one beauty, and that's Avery. Stepping closer, I reach around to gently loosen her ponytail and then run my fingers through the soft-as-silk strands. "I've wanted to do this since the day I first saw you."

"I've wanted to do this"—her palms reach around to squeeze my ass—"since the moment I saw you."

I mock gasp. "Avery Mills. What would the Playgroup moms think?"

She smirks. "They'd be right in line behind me."

My eyes drink in her perfect features—wide-set, glacier blue eyes, apple red round cheeks, Cupid's bow pink lips—while my fingers massage her scalp. She closes her eyes briefly, letting out a sigh. "That feels sooo good."

"That's my plan. To make you feel good."

I feel a twinge of guilt, knowing that I'm about to make love to a woman who isn't my wife. At the same time, I know I never felt as connected to Lisa as I do to Avery right now. "You're the first—the only—person I've been with in a long time," I whisper.

She blinks slowly, seeming to consider my words. "Thank you for telling me that."

Drawing her close, I brush my lips over hers, teasing and tasting. Taking my time for once. "I'm glad we got here early," I murmur between kisses. "I want to go slow. To get to know every bit of you."

"Sure you don't want to go zip-lining this afternoon instead? Little rock climbing?" Hands still on my butt, she pulls us closer so that my swiftly growing erection presses into her cleft.

"The only zipping I'm interested in is what it takes to get you out of these clothes." Palming her ass, I lift her to my hips. "And you're welcome to climb this rock as often as you like."

Groaning, she laughs at my dad joke. "What about horseback riding?"

"I think you know the answer to that question." Before she can taunt me further, I toss her onto the bed, stalking her as she scoots across it. When I pin her down with my torso, she squirms. I push away, thinking that I'm squashing her, but she loops her legs around my thighs. "I was just positioning myself for optimum..."

"Friction?" I finish for her.

"Exactly." She bites her lip and glances between us. "Except I think we need less fabric between us."

"I couldn't agree more." Levering up to my knees, I pull my button-down and t-shirt off in one swoop, but when I look down, she hasn't moved, so I reach for her zipper. "Okay?"

"I... just..." The pink on her cheeks spreads to the decolletage revealed by her blouse. "You said you didn't have a six-pack! You're jacked."

My own cheeks heat at the compliment, and my abdomen shivers when she strokes a finger over its ridges. "Working out keeps me sane."

When I reach for her buttons, she holds up a hand. "Just be forewarned. Things are far squishier under my clothes."

"I plan to worship at the altar of this body and its softness." Eyes on the prize, I make quick work of the shirt buttons before separating the flowery fabric to reveal a scrap of red lace cupping her breasts. Their pale curves are so inviting, my palms ache to replace the bra. As I trail a finger over it, I say, "I'm torn here—do I want you with or without lace?"

She squeezes my thighs with hers. "Maybe you should check out the matched set before removing it."

"Excellent plan."

"But first, there's the age-old question," she says, reaching for the button at the top of my khakis.

"Don't worry, I've got condoms."

She stills, blinking for a moment, before saying, "Well, that's good. But what I'm wondering is, boxers or briefs?"

The moment we reveal another bit red of lace on her and boxers on me, words in full sentences are no longer happening. All I can do is stroke and kiss my way from one end of her to the other. Her spine arches to meet my lips. Soft, pale skin shudders under my fingertips. But it's the little sounds she makes that really get me going—tiny whimpers, moans, and kitten-like growls.

Once we've lost the final bits of clothing, I fall to her side and play while she tells me where to touch and for how long. When her legs go rigid, I double down on her clit until she cries out, release rolling through her.

Watching her come down, my palm resting on her belly, she's so beautiful my throat tightens, full of so much feeling. Before I can ask if she needs anything, she swipes her hair out of her eyes and rolls on top of me.

"Where are those condoms? I need you inside me now."

"Uh... in my dopp kit?" My voice goes up in pitch at the end as I try not to laugh at her commanding tone.

She rolls off me again and points in the general direction of the door. "Go get 'em!"

After saluting her, I jog to my bag, glad there's a screen of trees and bushes outside the windows since all the curtains are wide open.

"And lube if you brought it," she calls after me.

"Copy that." Moments later, I'm back by her side with a handful of condoms and two kinds of lube. Holding them up, I say, "Water- or silicone-based?"

"I think water-based will work. I just want a little extra slipperiness. It's been a while."

She sits up, reaching for a condom and pressing a hand to my sternum. Following her lead, I fall onto my back and tuck my hands behind my head as she suits and then lubes me up. Draping her torso over mine, she balances on one arm while pressing my cock into her cleft with her other hand, rocking into me. My dick strains into her hand, begging for more, but before I can put words to its need, she shifts her hips and guides me to her entrance.

Holding my breath, I let her set the pace as she eases me in. "You okay?"

"More than okay. You feel so forking good." Her words end in a growly moan when she lands, her ass kissing my balls.

The combination of her goofy word choice with the sexy-as-hell throatiness of her voice—not to mention the way her walls grip my cock—has me grinning so hard my cheeks hurt. I've never had so much fun making love to a woman. Instead of dwelling on my past, I dive into the sensation, needing to savor every moment I get to be naked with Avery.

Words aside, she's not shy about finding her own pleasure, so when her fingers dip to her pussy, I egg her on. "I want to feel you come around me. Tell me what else you want."

"Your mouth on my breasts," she says, leaning over my torso.

My hands gather the soft globes, pushing them together so I can nuzzle between them before licking my way to one nipple while gently pinching the other.

"Harder," she says, her voice breathy, her cunt gripping me, engulfing me in sensation. As my cock drives into her wet warmth, she moans and gasps and mumbles half words and, finally, my name as another orgasm rocks through her.

Needing more friction, to be deeper inside, I flip us so I'm on top. Before entering again, I push her knees to the side, so she's spread wide for me. Just as I'm about to ask if she's okay, she reaches for my ass to pull me closer, moaning, "Yes."

And then I'm lost, unable to tell where she begins and I end or where the sounds of pleasure are coming from. I try to hang on to the feeling as long as I can, teetering on the edge. Wanting this to last forever as much as I want the release.

When climax comes, it's the sweetest reward.

The last thing I want to do is leave this extremely comfortable bed, especially because the sexiest woman I've ever been naked with is sharing it with me. But when a notification sounds from both of our phones, Avery rolls out of the nest. When I groan, she also holds out a hand to me. "We can always sneak out, but we have to at least show our faces."

Brushing wisps of her golden locks away from her face and cupping her cheeks, I lean in for what I truly intend to be a chaste kiss, but before I know it, my hands are roaming and my erection is back.

Until a very loud stomach growl echoes between us. "Was that me or you?"

She laughs, leaning away. "I don't know, but I do know there's food at tonight's meeting."

"I guess I could also use sustenance."

After patting me on the chest, she takes a step back and wags a finger at me. "No more touching, or we'll never get out of here."

"Fine."

After showering separately, we golf cart it to the dining hall where we're handed branded notebooks, an agenda, and a themed cocktail called Patio Season, a blend of Aperol, nocino, and sparkling wine. "Looks like we've got mingling time followed by the keynote and dinner," Avery says. "But I don't see our Irish friend."

I frown. "There's a brainstorming session after dinner."

Avery pats me on the arm. "Don't worry, we've got the whole weekend." Going up on tiptoes, she whispers in my ear, "Two whole nights. One cabin. One bed."

I should be networking, but I just end up following Avery around. She manages to make three new buddies over cocktails, and more at our assigned table for dinner. Jealousy curls through me, not wanting to share her with these strangers, but she looks so happy, so in her element, that I tamp it down. As she said, we've got two full nights together.

Keynote speakers at this kind of thing are rarely worth paying attention to. In my experience, it's either someone trying to sell you on something or an aging corporate leader who lost relevance years ago. I'm prepared to zone out and savor Avery's presence next to me, even if I can't pull her into my lap like I want, but the speaker's words eventually make it through the fog of lust.

"The dangers of a publicly owned and operated organization becoming dependent on a single privately-owned entity cannot be underestimated or ignored. Because private companies are subject to changes in leadership or corporate organization, even failure, public institutions cannot rely on a single private benefactor for support."

I'm wishing Eli were present, even as I note that it's probably a good thing that CPR seeks other funding sources.

When he talks about the benefits of collaboration and mentions social and environmental performance, I jot down a few notes. We've floated the idea of using the design of Trede's campus as part of a B-corp application. Perhaps a community partnership can be another piece of that puzzle.

He pauses meaningfully before wrapping up. "This kind of relationship should not be entered into without careful thought and planning. Plans should establish clear boundaries, build on a foundation of trust and shared goals, while maintaining openness to new possibilities."

I glance over at Avery, wondering if she's getting the same message I am. That we might learn some things about how to avoid pitfalls for our personal relationship here too. But before I can ask, she's off to the powder room with a few other women, telling me that she'll meet me in our small group session.

The session is specifically geared toward first-time PPP participants, and its leader—a tall woman with chestnut brown skin and a kind smile—encourages us to bring up anything we're concerned about. "What you're going through or worried about may be just what another person needs to hear," Regina Lowell says, her deep voice a balance of command and compassion.

After a few members of the group make comments, Avery raises her hand. As she did with the other individuals, Regina asks her to introduce herself and any colleagues present and to give the group a brief rundown of the project.

Avery does as asked, but when she's prompted to share her concerns, she side-eyes me before speaking. "There is an issue I've been avoiding."

"I'd love to facilitate this discussion, if you're willing," Regina says.

It takes me a moment to realize that she's talking to me. "Um, sure. Of course."

At Regina's urging, Avery continues. "We're collaborating on a reorganization at our rec center, and one of the programs I run is on the chopping block."

I can't suppress my responding wince, and Regina obviously notes it. "Mm-hmm. Is this coming from the corporate side or the community side?"

"Both, I suppose," Avery says with a quick glance at me. "The numbers don't support keeping the program. It takes up a large chunk of my time, and enrollment has dropped steadily over the past five years."

After nodding slowly for a moment, Regina turns to me. "Can I assume that you've been part of the discussion?"

"Yes," I say, wishing I'd made time to tell Avery my plan for Playgroup. "The budget is tight as it is, and there are some disagreements among stakeholders regarding prioritization."

"Always a challenge," Regina allows.

"But there are positives to Playgroup that you can't see in the numbers," Avery argues. "That you've experienced personally."

After teasing out the details of my experience and getting more input from Avery, Regina turns to the large pad of paper resting on an easel next to her and uncaps a magic marker.

"Let's make a list." She circles a finger around the room. "Working together, we might be able to find other ways to foster these elements."

Other members of the group begin throwing out ideas and Regina writes them down as she encourages us. "There are no dumb or wrong answers in this room."

"I also want to say that I've resisted cutting it because my mother started the program," Avery says at some point. "She's no longer able to lead it due to health issues."

"Personal attachment can make discussing change diffi-cult." Regina gives Avery an empathetic smile, before turning back to the group. "Perhaps we can find a way to hang on to the spirit of the program without bringing down the whole ship. To mix metaphors horribly."

"We should also consider..." The woman looks back and forth between me and Avery. "That as you're a couple on either side of this fence, as it were, that can bring additional challenges."

"Oh, we're—" Avery begins.

"Well aware of the challenges," I cut in, taking her hand. Avery's eyes narrow slightly, maybe trying to figure out what I'm up to. I'm not sure why I just outed us in front of these strangers, but I bring her hand to my lips for a quick kiss, hoping she's okay with it. "But we both want what's best for the community."

"And that's why we're here." Regina taps the easel. "Our goal is to create a sustainable architecture, so Climax Parks and Rec is not dependent on Trede in the long term. On the other hand, we want Trede and its stakeholders to feel their investment is being put to use wisely. And inclusively."

I'm pretty sure Trede's primary stakeholder wouldn't put it that way, but I would, so I nod. "I'm open to all suggestions. I want to make this work."

chapter
nineteen

AVERY

I love living in a small town, but there is something so invigorating about meeting new people. I'm not sure Josh feels the same, because at the end of the evening session, I'm definitely the only one following my new pals on social media and exchanging numbers. He seems impatient to get back to the room, and I am too, but before we get naked, we need to discuss a few things. So as soon as our golf cart is out of hearing range of the others, I let him know how I feel.

"I thought you said I could decide whether or not we're public about us."

He glances over at me briefly, and I catch the wince on his face as we pass under a lamppost. "I didn't really plan on it, but at that moment, it felt like I should put all the cards on the table so we get the best advice."

He has a point, but I'm still a little grumpy about it. "Or maybe you're just trying this on for size in a place where we don't know anybody."

"Maybe I was. Maybe that's why we need a weekend

away. Or two or three. So we can explore what's here without having to worry about our families."

"But those stressors are people. And they're not going anywhere."

"Believe me, I am aware of that. I have been since the moment my kids were born."

Pain thrums behind my sternum, making me even grumpier. Because I'll never have the feeling he's trying to get away from.

"Don't we deserve a little happiness, just for ourselves?" he continues. "Don't we need that, so we can fulfill our other responsibilities?"

He's right. It's what all the parenting books say. You can't be a caretaker without taking care of yourself. But I'm not ready to cede the point, so I remain stubbornly silent until he pulls up in front of the cabin.

After he turns off the cart, he shifts in his seat to face me. When I don't turn to face him, he takes my hand. "You make my life better, Avery. When I'm around you, I feel hopeful. I believe things will be okay. And I haven't felt like that in a long time."

Eyes on our joined hands, I ask, "Since Lisa passed?"

"Before that. I've been... lost, I think. So overwhelmed by trying to be the best partner to a woman who didn't want me, and a decent parent to children we hadn't planned for."

I let his words, as well as the real pain I hear in his voice, sink in for a moment. But it's when I finally meet his eyes that his hurt reaches inside my heart and pushes away the envy. Squeezing his hand, I ask, "Would you go back and change your choices? If you could?"

He shakes his head without hesitation. "I wouldn't give

up my kids for anything. I only wish they—Mabel, really—hadn't suffered because Lisa was so depressed, and I didn't know how to fix it."

"I'm not sure I—"

"You don't have to commit to anything right now, Avery. But I want you to know, if you're up for taking on my package deal, I want you in our life."

Hope of my own swirls around my heart, but something—I'm not sure what—has me holding back. "Let's... sleep on it?"

"If by sleep you mean let me make you come as many times as possible before we pass out, sated and satisfied, then my answer is yes."

How can I say no?

"There you are."

The next morning, when I look up from the desk where I've been scribbling away, it's confirmed. Josh is too good to be true. No one has the right to look as sexy as he does all sleep-rumpled and half-awake.

"Everything okay?" he asks.

I look down at the notebook I've filled with ideas. "Yes, actually."

He shuffles over and gives me a kiss on the side of my neck that's as sexy as it is sweet. "Did you sleep oka—" He veers past my shoulder to sniff my mug deeply. "Is that coffee?"

"Did you want some to drink or do the fumes just do it for you?"

"I like to start small," he says. "But if there's more

where that came from, I would be forever indebted to you."

Smiling as I think about how I might call that debt, I slip out of my chair and head for the kitchenette. As I'm pouring him a cup, I notice that he's just standing there, gazing out the window. "Did *you* sleep okay?"

His smile in answer is practically beatific. "I slept better than I have since... I have no idea how long."

When I hand him the mug, he takes a sip and then closes his eyes on a moan. "One, this is the best hotel coffee I've ever had. Two, how did you know how I like it?"

I bat my eyes as smugly as I can. "One, I brought my own beans and pour-over supplies. Two, I've had coffee with you. I've seen what you do to it." One tiny splash of milk and no sugar wouldn't work for me but I'm not here to judge people's coffee preferences.

"I feel like I'm still dreaming. And I was having such good dreams." The right side of his mouth quirks and his grin turns devilish. "You had starring roles in all of them."

He sets down his mug and opens his arms wide. I take the invitation, snuggling into his chest as he wraps his arms around me tight. "Humans need eight hugs a day. I read that recently."

"I don't think I've been getting enough."

"We need to do something about that."

"Are you saying you'll take responsibility for my eight daily hugs?"

"I'd like to." His hands roam down my back. "I'd like to take on all of your hug-related needs."

"Like kisses?"

He levers back to answer my question with a slow, sensual kiss.

"You're hired."

"What about caresses?"

I tap my chin, pretending to consider. "Hmm... Let's see what you've got."

When he scoops me up and heads for the bedroom, I let out an ear-piercing squeal of shock. "What are you doing?"

"Showing you what I've got, of course."

It's a good thing I got up early because he takes his time teasing me with his hands and mouth before driving me right to the edge with a joystick that was made for my console. After an equally enjoyable shared shower, he leaves me to my makeup application while he checks in on his family. But when I emerge, ready to head to breakfast and morning workshops, he's reading my scribblings.

"Is this what you were working on this morning?" he asks.

Straightening the papers, feeling self-conscious about them, I say, "I just woke up thinking about what Regina said last night. About figuring out how to keep the spirit of Playgroup without getting dragged down by what doesn't work."

He turns to face me, propping a hip on the desk. "I was going to make it a surprise, but my current proposal includes Playgroup. You've sold me on its value. I was able to move some line items around so—"

"What if I don't want to keep it?"

"But I thought you—"

"It's my mother's program," I say.

"Her legacy, right. I know. Another reason to keep it."

I shake my head, my determination growing. "Nothing lasts forever. Cutting it won't change her impact over the years."

"But..." His brow furrows. "You're so good at it. With the kids and the par—"

"I'm not a parent," I say, the words coming out more forcefully than I intend. But instead of reining them in, I just keep going. "It's all theoretical to me. It's ridiculous for me to offer advice when I don't know anything about the challenges people are facing. Trying to empathize with their complaints and frustrations when I can't even—"

"But you're young. You could have kids. You have plenty of time."

"Pfft. Time I've got. What I lack is the plumbing."

"Plumbing?"

"I can't. Have kids. There. Now you know."

Josh just stares at me.

"I'm not sure how we got from morning orgasms to arguing about Playgroup to this but now that we're here, if you're really thinking you want to"—I make air quotes—"make this work, then you should know what you're getting into."

Before I lose the nerve, I tell him the story of my salpingectomy, leaving out the gaslighting from the dillweed doctor and that son of a biscuit Peter. Then, before he can tell me that he's no longer interested, avoiding what is sure to be either a look of pity or disgust in his eyes, I beat it out the door. "I think I need a walk. I'll see you later."

We'd already planned to split up for the morning, to cover as many workshops as possible. Last night, I'd resisted because I wanted to spend as much time as possible together, but Josh argued that if we covered more ground, we could skip the afternoon's so-called "bonding" activities, which he said were usually lame.

I skip breakfast, needing time to walk off the agitation. The feeling of being exposed. I attend the first workshop, but I don't have a clue what it's about, because even though I sit there and take notes, my mind is churning. Trying, and failing, to convince myself that I did the right thing. After all, if Josh really wants more kids, it's better to end it now. Before I get too attached.

As if that hasn't happened already.

At the second workshop, I linger in the hallway, pretending I'm not looking for him. But when they begin to introduce the speaker, I make myself slip into the back row where I can stew in peace. But just as the lights lower for the visual presentation, someone sits next to me. Someone who smells of pine, with a faint undertone of baby wipes.

He takes my hand in both of his. When I make myself look at him, even in the dim light, I can tell there's no pity or revulsion in his light blue eyes.

Just hope.

"I know we said we'd split up, but I couldn't pay attention," he whispers. "I just kept thinking about how good you are with kids. How hard it must be to work with parents who don't appreciate what they have."

The person in front of us turns around to give us a pointed look, but Josh just scoots closer. "Thank you for telling me. Things haven't changed for me. I'm still all in."

I just squeeze his hand for a long moment, swallowing back the tears clogging my throat. But I eventually manage to whisper back, "Me too."

I'm not sure if it's being away from my day-to-day routine, having told Josh about my past, or the many ways we've made each other feel good in the past twenty-four hours, but I've never felt so inspired and alive. Like all the ways I've pretended to be happy for the past few years were just a rehearsal for the real thing. After the morning sessions, we're told to dress for physical activities for the afternoon. Changing clothes back at the cabin, it's tempting to skip lunch for a quickie, but we decide that we'll enjoy everything better with fuel in our bellies.

I've been so impressed with all the presenters so far, but when the speaker steps up to the podium at lunch, I gasp.

Josh looks over at me. "Something wrong?"

I shake my head. "It's her. The Dubliner we gave the room to."

According to the man who introduces her, Frances O'Leary is a world-renowned expert on play. When she steps away from the podium to stroll across the stage, I know that what we're going to get from her is a TED talk, only better. Because of her charming accent, of course.

She talks for a bit about her early research on human development and play, as well as her most recent work on its health benefits for all ages. But then she turns the tables on us.

"Why? Are? You? Here?" she asks, emphasizing each word equally. In her lovely accent.

Josh snorts, and my cheeks heat when I catch his eye. "Besides nookie," I whisper.

"Why do you work in this field?" Frances O'Leary continues. "Or if you're here from the corporate side, what do you gain from contributing to this work? I know it's not money, believe me."

She nods offstage, and a large whiteboard gets rolled out. "We're going to find out."

They're really into brainstorming at this place, but this is next level from what we did last night. When Frances gets people shouting out a few words, they appear on the board like magic. Then she tells us to get out our phones, and she gives us a number to which we'll send a text.

"Why are you here?" she repeats. "What is the value of a public place where people can enjoy parks and recreation?"

She gives us a few moments to think, sweeping the room with one of those gazes that makes you feel like she's talking to you, and I swear the entire room holds its breath. "When I say *go*, I want every one of you to type in and send the first ten words that come to mind in response to that question. Aaand, go!"

I dutifully type in my words, doing my best not to edit them. When I look up, the whiteboard is pulsing with words. Some of which were on my list, some of which weren't. When it seems like the board might overflow with them, the words begin to swirl, and after a few seconds, a word cloud appears.

The ones I fall in love with are:

Community

Fun

Inspiration

Connection

Re-creation

"You'll all get a printout of this before you leave, and I recommend putting it by your computer or somewhere you'll see it every day. So you'll have a memory of what's behind your hard work. And this afternoon."

Her tone is almost mischievous when she gets to the last sentence, and then she gives us a wave and shouts, "Have fun!" before handing the mic off to a staff member.

"If you didn't dress to play," the man says, "I highly recommend doing so now. You're likely to get dirty, and you need to be able to move all your limbs easily. But before anyone leaves, please reach under your chair and retrieve the sticky note placed there. That's your team color. No trading now," he warns with a smile. "Please gather by the flag in your team color on the playing fields in fifteen minutes."

Josh holds up his sticky note. "I guess we're not on the same team."

"Classic move," I say as we join the lines snaking out of the building. "Separate people sitting together to break up the cliques."

"How are we playing this?" he asks, gesturing for me to precede him through the door.

"I don't know about you, but I play to win."

He grins. "Good to know."

Once out on the playing field, however, I'm wishing I hadn't thrown that gauntlet.

"Maybe the challenges will be more intellectual?" one of my team members suggests. She's a librarian and looks the part, in sensible shoes and a cardigan. At least she's wearing a skort instead of a tweed skirt.

"Doubt it." The art teacher in our group is tall but not muscular. They frown as they point toward the center of the field, revealing a beautiful sleeve of tattoos. "First contest looks like it's tug-of-war."

Scanning the field, it seems that jocks are well represented, but if I were to categorize the members of my team into high school categories, we're limited to geeks and artsy types. Only one of us looks the least bit athletic, and she can't be more than five feet tall.

The petite dance and yoga teacher groans as she gathers her locs into a ponytail. "This isn't fai—"

Her complaint is interrupted by the blowing of a whistle. "Before we begin, I want to clarify a few points," the staff member says through a bullhorn. "One, we are well aware that the team makeup may not seem fair, but we've found that in the end, random groups serve the learning process."

The art teacher snorts. "Learning process, my ass."

"Two," the guy with the bullhorn continues, "each member of the winning team earns a one-on-one consultation with Dr. O'Leary and gets to be first in line at dinner tonight."

"Great," Tisha, the dance teacher, mutters. "My community center could really use that consult. But we have no hope of winning."

"Three," Bullhorn man says, "we will provide gloves for tug-of-war."

"Thank goodness." An IT guy on my team pushes his glasses up the bridge of his nose. "You can get serious rope burns from those things."

"Fourth and final point." The bullhorn squawks. "The winning team will be the team that has the most fun, no matter the actual outcome of the challenges."

IT guy snorts. "Sorry, kids, but none of this is fun for me."

"What would be fun for you?" I ask.

"Seriously?"

"Yeah."

"Taking a nap. My cabinmate snores like you wouldn't believe and I got no rest last night."

I scan the area and notice a few chairs set up along the sidelines. "Why don't you take a load off? Maybe you can catch a catnap."

He frowns. "But then you'll be short a player."

"It's not like we're going to win the tug-of-war," the tattooed art teacher called Atlas says. "You may as well sit it out."

"But I want to win this," Tisha insists.

"Did you not hear what the man said?" the librarian asks. "The winners are the ones who have fun. So if it's more fun for him to sit on the sideline, that's what he should do."

"They didn't really mean that, though," Atlas scoffs.

"It's what they said," the IT guy says with a shrug. "I'm taking them at their word."

"Who gives a shiitake mushroom, anyway?" I say. "It's a beautiful day, and we're away from it all in this gorgeous place. If we have fun, that's a win anyway."

"So we just give up?" Tisha asks. "Let ourselves be pulled across the line?"

"Actually," I say. "I have an idea."

twenty

JOSH

When Avery's team, aptly named The Toddlers, wins the tug-of-war by making their opponents laugh so hard that they can't breathe, I'm pretty sure I know whose idea it was to sing "If You're Happy and You Know It" at the top of their lungs the entire time they pulled on the rope. If I didn't already know it was her favorite song to lead in Playgroup, I can tell by the triumphant grin on her face.

Her ingenuity and natural leadership work for her team for the rest of the activities too. And it even seems to set the tone for the rest of the participants. Sure, the staff told us that the team having the most fun would win, but no one in my group, uncreatively named Team Green, took that seriously. Until we took on The Toddlers in life-size checkers. The combination of having to leapfrog over our opponents while listening to Avery's trash talk—made funnier by her creative non-swear words—had us all laughing our asses off.

The relaxed atmosphere lends itself well to paddleboat races too, especially when Team WTF—taking a page from Avery's book—speeds to the win by chanting "Ee-oh-ee-oh" ala the guards in *The Wizard of Oz*.

But the pièce de résistance is Paint Twister. When I go splat in the gooey finger paint, instead of feeling defeat, I roll off the mat until my clothes look like some kind of deranged Rorschach test and then launch at my teammates, hugging them until they're covered too.

I've never had more fun in my entire life.

And then I think of something that would be even more fun.

Avery is slightly less paint covered than I am, so she drives us back to the cabin. On the way, I share my current concern with her. "I think we really need to think about conserving water."

She shoots me a look like, *I see where you're going with this.* "I'm not sure showering together will actually save water."

"You could be right." Since I'm not behind the wheel, I just watch the woman next to me, imagining stripping her slowly.

"What?" She glances over at me briefly. "What's going on over there?"

I point ahead. "Eyes on the road, missy. We need to get to the cabin in one piece if I'm going to get you clean."

She keeps her gaze forward, but the way she squirms in the seat has me raring to go. The minute she parks the cart, I'm on my feet. Before hers hit the ground, I'm scooping her up off the seat. She squeals in protest as I carry her up the steps, but she has the key out of her bag and the door open before I can ask, and her head nestles into my shoulder with a sigh as I carry her over the threshold and kick the door shut behind me.

I get the shower going and strip us both out of our paint-sticky clothes. She steps in first, moaning with pleasure under the warm spray, but when she reaches for the shampoo, I ask, "May I take it from here?"

Her eyes spark as she turns to face me, and when she hands me the bottle, she holds up her hands as if in surrender. "It's all yours. My hair is a pain in the bus."

"How dare you insult these golden tresses?" I ask with mock indignation. "We'll just have to lather, rinse, and repeat until you can appreciate them."

I tip up her chin and protect her eyes while I wet her hair. After I add a big dollop of the rosemary scented hotel shampoo and work it through the soft strands, I begin to massage her scalp.

She groans, her hand reaching for the wall.

"Too much?"

"Just right," she says on an exhale. "Feels so good."

I only rinse and repeat one time, but after we scrub off the paint splotches, I nestle her back to my front, encourage her to lean against me, and caress her seam and clit and breasts while the water rains down until she cries out and the waves of a climax rock through her.

And then I dry her off and take her to bed to do it all over again, but this time, I fill her with everything I've got.

It's not easy to separate my naked body from hers, but our stomachs talk us into returning to the larger group for dinner. On the drive over, Avery worries about her hair looking a mess, but no one seems to notice. Instead, her team drags her to their winning spot at the front of the dinner line. Instead of following, I do a little networking. After another inspiring keynote, this time from a CEO passionate about his work with his community partners, conversation flows as we each share what we've learned.

After dinner, we break out into small groups again, but this time I'm in a group with others from the private sector. It's refreshing to see how many in upper management really believe in the upsides of making their communities better places to live. I offer a few ideas, but mostly I'm jotting down notes, soaking up my peers' experiences like the heart-shaped sponge I toss into my kids' bath.

Later, Avery and I make love again and then just lie there talking about anything and everything until our words come further and further apart and we relax into sleep.

chapter
twenty-one

AVERY

Sunday morning, I somehow wake up horny. I can't count the number of big O's I've enjoyed this weekend, because every time we're alone, there's touching and talking that turns me on. I just wish this feeling could last.

In college, there were just too many men to meet. I didn't want to stick with just one, so things were always exciting and new. Later, when Peter and I decided to move in together, things got routine pretty quickly. I figured that's what happens. You trade novel and thrilling for trusted and ordinary.

It's hard to imagine that happening with Josh, though. Something about him makes me want to try new things. Take risks. And not just here in bed, but at work and in the rest of my life.

"You know," the man of my thoughts murmurs next to me, "I have to admit something."

My gut tenses for a moment, ready for the shoe to drop. But when he nuzzles into my back, the fear dissipates, and I turn to face him. "Tell me. I can take it."

A half grin lifts one side of his mouth, like he's not quite awake enough to work both sides. His hand curves over my waist to caress my hip, circling over my bum to dip between my cheeks. My leg loops over him of its own accord until I'm straddling him, rocking my needy center into his growing erection.

Josh's grin is now symmetrical, but he's obviously still half in dreamland as I work him over, running my nails over his abs—not a six-pack maybe, but definitely a four—before following with my torso. His expression is so blissful, I want to keep him in this state, so instead of moving up his body to kiss him awake, I move down, following the happy trail.

When I fist him, his shaft jumps. When I take the head between my lips, his hips lift off the bed.

"Aaaverrreee," he moans. A quick glance confirms that his smile has only grown wider, so I continue my exploration, playing his flute with my lips, teeth, tongue, and fingers.

Who knew that skill sets learned in marching band could pay off later in life?

When I take him fully into my mouth, he grabs the sheets. When I pump him with my hand and lave the head with my tongue, his hips roll. But when I combine the two, increasing speed, he growls, "I'm gonna come, sweetheart."

He tries to pull me up his body, but I swat him away. I want to feel this, I want to take him there. He gives up the protest pretty quickly, and I speed things up, finding a rhythm, and then he's pistoning into my mouth and hand. My walls clench like he's inside me and when he spurts into my mouth, I'm shuddering too, pleasure shooting through me as I swallow.

Sometime later, after I've collapsed next to him and am snuggled into his chest, I remember that he was going to admit to something before I ravished him. "What was it you were going to tell me before?"

His brow furrows for a moment. "Oh. I remember now. It's just that... your willingness to be adventurous has surprised me this weekend." His voice raspy, he says, "After we... you know... on the phone."

Laughing, I whap him with a pillow. "Josh Harmon. If this girl can say the word sex, you can too."

"Well, that's my point. You don't swear, and when we had *phone sex*"—he leans close and overarticulates the words—"I did most of the talking. So I kind of thought you'd be... I don't know, timid in bed."

I purse my lips and consider his words. "The word thing is separate from sex for me, for one thing. As for the phone sex, I was working so hard to picture you while feeling everything so much, I don't think I could've formed a sentence."

He traces a finger over the curve of my shoulder. "I would've been happy to explore this body any way you wanted. But it's been an extra bonus to watch you let loose."

I want to talk about what happens next, but we only have an hour before we have to check out. So I roll on top of him, capture his lips with mine for a savoring kiss, and then whisper, "Last one to the shower's a rotten egg."

Between the notes I took, the ideas we brainstormed, and the contact info for people I hope to continue to collaborate with—not to mention the consult I have scheduled with Frances O'Leary—my Wildwood Retreat Center notebook is almost full by the time we pack up the car and head down the drive. Kind of like me: my belly's full of an amazing breakfast, my body's more sexually sated than it's ever been, and my heart is full of hope for the future.

I'm a teensy bit nervous about what'll happen when we get back to the real world, but for now, staring out the window as the trees and meadows and hills and streams and farmhouses and quaint downtown streets roll by, Josh's free hand resting on my thigh, I'm happy to put it off as long as possible.

Josh seems much less concerned about what awaits back at home. "I want to tell my parents about us first, then I think Mabel." He sets his right hand on the console between us, palm up. "What do you think the kids should call you?"

"Are you sure it's not too early?" I counter. "I just don't want them to be confused."

"Confused by what?"

"Well, they've only ever had a mom, right? From what you've said it sounds like you haven't brought home any girlfriends."

His lips press together in thought. "Maybe just Avery. Although, I guess Percy should still call you Miss Avery in class."

"See?" I give his hand a squeeze. "It's a little confusing."

"No more than if you *were* his mom. I mean, if you were his teacher, he wouldn't call you mommy in class."

"If I were his mom, I wouldn't also be his teacher."

"Good point," he allows, squeezing me back. "I'm not worried. We'll figure it out."

Startling awake, it takes me a moment to figure out where I am, but when Josh says, "Hi, Mom. I'm on the way home," and I look out the window to see the Hudson flowing by, I relax back into my seat, determined to savor the rest of the time alone with him.

"How far away are you?" Frieda's voice is tinny in the car speakers, but the panic in her tone has me sitting up straight.

Josh glances at the navigation screen. "Just about thirty minutes, but we were thinking of stopping for lun—"

"Oh, thank god," his mother says.

"Is something wrong?"

"Well, yes. I'm so sorry and I don't know how this happened but... Mabel is missing."

The car swerves slightly and Josh goes white as a sheet. "She's what?"

I lean closer to him and grip the steering wheel. "Frieda, this is Avery. I'm going to get Josh to pull over."

"We need to get home," Josh says, wild-eyed.

"We need to get home in one piece. Let me drive so you can focus on what your mom is saying."

"Fine," he says, before swerving onto the shoulder.

Grabbing the panic bar, I tell myself that it's a good thing we're no longer on one of the cliff-hugging mountain roads. Moments later, I'm driving, and Josh has disconnected the call from the car. Part of me wants to ask if he can put it on speaker so I can hear too, but it's now my job to get us home—well, back to his parents' house, anyway —safely.

"Okay. Don't worry, Mom. It's not your fault. These things happen." He leans over to peer at the map. "We're close. I'll see you soon. Love you too."

He disconnects the call and when I glance over, he's just staring straight ahead.

"What happened?"

His fist is at his mouth, flexing around his phone so hard that the veins on the back of his hand stick out. "I fucked up."

"What do you mean?"

"I can't leave these kids. They're too young. My parents are too old to take care of them."

My heart skitters around in my chest like it's looking for a place to hide. "What happened, Josh?"

When he doesn't answer, I glance over again. He's still staring straight ahead, his jaw flexed like he's grinding his teeth. I reach over to try and squeeze his shoulder, but he bats my arm away. "Mabel's lost, okay? Apparently, the cat got out early this morning and they all went looking for her. After knocking on doors in the neighborhood, they went back to the house and then"—he breaks off, his nostrils flaring, lips pressed together—"and then my parents realized Mabel wasn't with them."

"She went looking for Jenny Linsky by herself," I say softly.

"Seems like that's what happened, yeah," he says, his tone so sharp with sarcasm that I flinch. "My mom was so flustered I couldn't get more out of her. They called the police, so"—he blows out a shaky breath—"I guess that's good."

Just as I'm about to say something inane like I'm so sorry this happened, he slams his hand onto the dashboard. "Fuck!"

I can't know what he's feeling. I'll never know. But I'm sure he's regretting going away this weekend and now is not the time to remind him that self-care is important for parents. So I put all my attention on getting us back to Climax as quickly and safely as possible.

The minute we turn onto his street, we see the flashing lights of police cars. They're in the driveway and in front of the house, so I have to stop in the middle of the street. Before I can tell him that he can get out and I'll park the car, he swears again.

"What is it?"

He stares at an older couple talking to his parents on the front lawn. "Lisa's parents are here." His head shaking, he mutters, "This was such a fucking mistake."

And then, without even looking at me, he gets out of the car and sprints for the house.

Josh's words echo in my ears as I watch him embrace his mother on their front lawn. He is right. The children should be his first priority. I'd hoped to be by his side instead of another mistake in his life, but *my* life has proven that you can't always get what you want.

Clearly, there's no place for me here, but it's not until a policeman tells me that I need to move out of the way that I realize I don't have a way to leave, because I left my own car at CPR for the weekend. After parking Josh's car as close to the house as I can, I get out and search up and down the street. As I wonder if I can catch a ride to my car with a safety officer, I realize that people are gathering around a fire truck.

As I draw near, a firefighter holds up a map with a section outlined in red. "You here to search?"

Fire truck. Jenny Linsky. *Pickles.*

Instead of taking the map, I turn around and run to the house, bits and pieces from Mabel's collection of Cat Club books connecting like a puzzle in my brain. In *The School for Cats*, Jenny is sent away from New York City to live in the country. Just like we did, Mabel told me.

Without even knocking, I slip through the Harmons' front door and head for the living room, where I immediately find clues to support my theory: an abandoned toy fire truck and sooty cat pawprints near the fireplace and then heading out of the room. I can just picture Mabel looking up the chimney for her frightened cat and then following her prints out the door.

Needing confirmation, I follow the sound of voices to the kitchen, but I hesitate just outside the room, my hunch suddenly feeling ridiculous. What will I say? *Excuse me, but I think the lost child is re-enacting the plot from a story book?*

Yeah, no. They'd laugh in my face.

Stepping away from the kitchen, I head for the back door instead.

In the book, after falling out of the chimney and escaping outdoors, Jenny Linsky goes on quite a few adventures. As night falls, she ends up in a forest. Kind of like the one behind the Harmons' house. It's getting darker and chillier by the minute, so I click the flashlight app on my phone and step into the woods.

Twenty minutes later, after tripping over yet another root and landing painfully on my knees, I'm ready to give up. After all, Bert Harmon probably searched this area before the sun went down. The police would've too. Why should I think I'd do a better job just because I read a children's book?

Typical.

Turning around, trying to figure out which direction will take me back to the house, I hear a soft mew.

Stock still, I close my eyes, hoping the sound will come again. But instead of another cat noise, I hear, "Shh, Jenny."

"Mabel?" I whisper.

Silence for a few beats, then, "Miss Avery?"

"It's me," I say, keeping my voice soft. "Did you find Jenny?"

"I did," Mabel says, her voice cracking. "But now I'm stuck. And I'm afraid."

"Of the fox?" In the story, Jenny Linksy climbs the tree to get away from a scary fox in the forest.

"I didn't see the fox," Mabel whispers. "I'm afraid of the police."

It doesn't seem like the time to try and convince her otherwise, so I ask, "What part of you is stuck?"

"My foot. It hurts." The tears behind her words grab on to my heart, and before I know it, I'm halfway up the tree.

I'm also regretting all my life decisions, from never taking up rock climbing to the tight jeans I put on this morning, which make it even more difficult to get my buttinski up this forking tree. But every whimper from Mabel and every plaintive mew from the cat spurs me on.

Eventually, I've got myself wedged between some branches just below them.

But when I try to dislodge Mabel's foot, she squeals in pain.

"Sorry, sorry, sorry." Gently pushing a few strands of hair out of her eyes, I murmur, "How about we call your dad?"

Mabel shivers, but it's hard to tell if it's from the chill in the air or fear. "Just not the firemen or the police."

"But honey, firemen are experts at getting cats out of trees."

"But she's scared of Pickles the fire cat!"

"I know," I say softly. "But what if we told them to take off their hats?"

She's quiet for a moment. "And their uniforms?"

"Got it. No scary uniforms."

Thankfully, Josh answers my call, and I launch right into a brief explanation of where we are and what Jenny Linksy and Mabel are afraid of. He says he'll work it out with the officers and as soon as we hang up, I drop a pin with our location and text it to him.

There's no getting comfortable up here, so I focus on distracting both of us while we wait. "Tell me the story of how you found Jenny."

chapter
twenty-two

JOSH

"Home is the place for me."

This line from the cat book is on repeat in my head as Mabel retells her story for the third or fourth time. A very different tale than the one I've been living for the past couple of hours. To Mabel, she's the hero who figured out that Jenny Linsky would end up in the woods, because that's what city cats who've been sent away to live in the country do. Mabel is the one who knew to be quiet and listen for her cat rather than yelling the cat's name. She knew that Jenny Linsky would feel frightened and alone. Only she could save her.

I couldn't save her mother, but she could save her cat.

"Plus, Jenny Linsky found me when I got lost, so I owed her," Mabel says proudly from her spot on the couch, her ankle swaddled in ice packs the EMTs gave us.

Shit. Of course Mabel would bring this up and give my in-laws yet another reason to find me an unfit father.

"Do you mean when you got lost today?" my mother asks.

"No, Nana. In New York."

"You got lost in New York City?" Jack Kingston asks, justifiably horrified.

"It was in the apartment building," I clarify.

"I was outside, Daddy."

"You were in the back courtyard, not wandering around the city."

She turns to her grandparents, animated again. "I didn't like the nanny who came after Percy was born. She didn't want to play at all. She just wanted to hold Percy. So I decided to go to the playground by myself."

"This nanny was fired the next day," I add. "Lisa had just returned to work, so I took parental leave and stayed home with the kids instead."

Jack frowns, obviously judging my choices, because when my leave was up, I quit the job he likely pulled strings to get me. I couldn't leave the kids in the hands of a stranger again.

"How did the cat find you?" Tilly Kingston asks.

"I knew how to get to the playground. Take the elevator, go out the door, and walk two blocks. But when I got off the elevator and went out the door, everything looked different. Plus, the door locked behind me. I was sitting there very mad, and Jenny Linsky walked up and comforted me."

As Mabel goes on to reconnect this story back to today's debacle, my brain replays the panic I felt when I got the call from Lisa that day telling me that I had to go home to find Mabel.

I can't do it, Josh, she said. *I just returned to work, and they'll think I'm not serious if I go running home every time there's a little problem.*

Like losing our child in fucking Manhattan was a little problem.

"And then Miss Avery climbed the tree," Mabel's voice in the here and now pierces the memory. "She knew where Jenny Linksy would be too, and she knew to be quiet, but she also had a cell phone."

My head jerks up, and I scan the faces of the people gathered in the cozy living room listening to my daughter's story. Both sets of grandparents are here, along with a few neighbors who helped search for my daughter. But Avery isn't among them.

Mabel may have saved her cat, but Avery is the one who found Mabel. The person who paid attention to my daughter and guessed what she might be thinking. Who was able to reassure her when my little girl was convinced that the fireman would frighten the cat.

Avery is the one missing now.

And who can blame her? I freaked out when I saw my in-laws. I don't even know what I said. All I could think was that I was being punished for every moment I'd enjoyed with her.

I failed. Again.

And Lisa's parents were there to judge me. Again.

It's late by the time we get the kids settled for the night. The Kingstons haven't jumped down my throat yet; they even insisted on getting dinner delivered. But by bedtime, Percy is wound up from being stuck inside most of the day, while Mabel has a major tantrum when I try to get her to take a bath.

By the time the kids fall asleep, I want to crawl into bed too. Preferably with the woman who keeps sending me direct to voicemail. I have to force myself to go back downstairs where I'm sure to get a dressing down from Lisa's parents.

But the only person waiting up for me is my mom.

"Where is everybody?"

My mom looks up from the Sunday crossword. "The Kingstons went to their hotel and your dad went to bed."

"I was sure they'd have a lawyer here, ready to make me sign over custody."

My mom frowns. "What are you talking about?"

I shrug. "They've been waiting for me to screw up ever since Lisa died. Ready to swoop in and take my"—a wave of emotion hits me out of nowhere and I have to swallow it back—"our kids."

"Oh, honey." My mom gets up and comes around the island to wrap her arms around me. She's tall for a woman, but she feels smaller than she used to somehow. "They wouldn't do that. Even if they could. They want what's best for Mabel and Percy."

"Problem is, their idea of best is a little different from mine."

My mom gives me a final squeeze. "How about some herbal tea?"

I sink onto a barstool. "Sure. That'd be great."

As she bustles about, my mom hums. It takes me a few moments to realize that it's a song Avery leads at Playgroup. When she sets a steaming mug in front of me, I just stare at it.

"That was some impressive detective work on Avery's

part today," she says after a beat. "But then she disappeared so fast."

I just nod.

Her head tips to the side. "Did something happen with you two? Over the weekend?"

Only that I fell in love with her and then fucked everything up.

Not that I'm going to say that to my mom.

"We, uh, had a good weekend. Productive. And we talked about going public as a couple going forward but I'm not sure it's a good idea."

"Why not?"

"She's just, you know, got a lot going on. And I have the kids..."

My mom places a hand on my arm. "Sweetheart. Lisa would want you to be happy."

I snort. "I doubt that. She was never happy with me. No matter what I did, I couldn't make her happy." Emotion clogs my throat again and I scrub a hand over my face. "I can't—I can't fail like that again."

My hands grip the mug in front of me. I have a sudden urge to throw it across the room, scalding liquid and all. But acting on impulse hasn't exactly served me lately, so I force myself to be still.

"Josh, honey, look at me."

Swallowing past the boulder in my throat, I do as she asks.

"Josh, do you think Lisa's death was your fault?"

Eyes back on the tea, I shrug. "Maybe not that actual incident, and I don't think she meant to end her life, but she was depressed. Severely depressed. Nothing I did made a difference, so I threw myself into work and then into taking care of the kids. I couldn't take care of her too."

My mom takes in a breath like she's going to say something, but I just keep going, needing to get this out. "I feel like I can't do all the things. It's either be a good employee or a good partner or a good father. If I take my eye off the ball, everything falls apart, so I have to choose. And being a good partner seems like the one that has to go. So, yeah. Things aren't going to work with me and Avery."

She waits a beat or two and then asks, "If things were different, would you want to be with her? With Avery?"

"Of course I would. Avery is amazing. She's smart and funny and gorgeous and... people love her."

One corner of her mouth lifts in a half smile she passed down to me. "*People* love her?"

"That's what I said," I growl.

She takes a long sip of her tea, and I do the same, hoping it'll calm me down. And it does, a little. Or maybe it's just comforting to sit here in the quiet with my mom, knowing that my kids are safe upstairs. "I guess I'll never know if Lisa and I would've lasted."

"You have a chance for a fresh start, Josh."

Gripping the mug again, I make myself ask, "What if the same thing happens all over again?"

My mom reaches across the counter, pries the empty mug away from me, and pushes it to the side before gripping both my hands. "Josh, I want you to hear this. You are the only person whose happiness you can control. If you can accept that, model that, it's the greatest gift you can give your children. Self-love and acceptance."

Oh yeah, I'll get right on that, is what I want to say, but I just nod.

"Have you ever noticed where a juggler looks?"

I just shake my head, too tired to follow this logic.

My mom straightens and points at me. "You said you can't take your eye off the ball. But a juggler doesn't keep his eye on one ball. His eyes remain straight ahead while the balls circle around him. His peripheral vision keeps track of their movement. He trusts that all the practice he's done will pay off, that his hands know what to do."

When I just stare at her, not sure what exactly she means, she points at me again. "You know what to do. You just have to trust yourself."

chapter
twenty-three

AVERY

It feels like the idyll in the Berkshires happened months ago, even though it's been only two and a half days since Josh whisked me away for the weekend.

My body doesn't seem to realize that things are over between us, because it's completely immune to the charms of the guy who gives me a ride back to the CPR parking lot. The one we all call the Hot Fireman.

When he asks if I want to get a beer, I just give him a limp wave. "No thanks, Jared, I'm beat."

He winks and shoots a finger gun at me. "I'll take a rain check, then."

Besides mine, there's one other car in the employee lot: Daisy's ancient Ford Bronco. The center closes at six on Sundays, so it's a little odd that she's still here. I called home to tell my mom I'd be late as soon as we found Mabel, and she reassured me that they were all set for dinner, so they won't be left high and dry if I check on my friend.

There's no way I was going to Come Again with Jared,

but a chat with Daisy feels like just the ticket. Some distraction before I head back to my childhood room to face the fact that I'm cursed when it comes to love, no matter what the darn clock thinks.

The center is locked up and the lights are off, but the minute I step inside, I hear music. Following the sound, I turn the corner to see light spilling from the art room doorway, and when I step inside, I find Daisy dancing around the room holding a paintbrush like it's a microphone. The tune is infectious, the lyrics are hopeful—something about the good outweighing the bad in life—and I'm enraptured by the sight of my friend throwing her entire self into singing along with what I'm pretty sure is the Barenaked Ladies.

Until she notices me. After turning down the music, she asks, "Are you crying?"

I swipe away what may in fact be tears from my cheeks. "No."

"Oh, well. That's good. Must be allergies."

"Yep. That's it. Allergies."

Her head tips to the side. "What are you doing here?"

"What are *you* doing here?"

"Painting," she says, like *obviously*. "I mean, just now I was taking a dance break, but I always paint on Sunday nights. It's the only time I can get lost in it, you know? With nobody here."

"Can I see?"

"Sure." She points the paintbrush at me. "No judgies, though. Creativity in progress and all that."

The very large square piece of wood on her easel is painted in bold geometrics in the shape of a star. Or maybe a flower. "Is this a barn quilt?"

She nods, seeming to be happy that I get it. "My version of it, anyway."

"What do you mean?"

"Well, usually, they're just paint on wood so they can be hung on the side of a barn. But mine are more like collages."

When I step closer, I can see that while she's painted the underlying shapes, she's added things on top. Pieces of fabric and old newspapers and even small items like drawer pulls and shells and feathers.

"The dumb thing is, now I can't sell them to hang on barns because the elements would ruin them. So I don't know what to do with them, but I can't seem to stop making them."

"It's beautiful," I say, entranced by the way she's echoed the paint colors with the objects. "If a little eerie."

Daisy clasps her hands and bounces on her toes. "That's exactly what I was going for!"

"You sure you can't sell them? Like, for inside art?"

"Do you know how much work it takes to sell art? Apply for a spot in some little show? Or set up an Etsy where nobody wants to pay for shipping?" She shrugs. "I just do it for me, anyway."

We stare at the piece for a few moments. I've just noticed what looks like an eyeball from a stuffed animal when she asks, "So, how was the weekend?"

"Oh." I shrug. "Fine."

She pokes me with the wooden end of her brush. "Doesn't sound fine. You seem mad."

I shake my head. "I'm not mad."

"Are you sure? You look mad."

I cross my arms over my chest. "I'm not mad."

"Whatever you say."

"Okay, I'm forking mad!" I even throw my arms in the air and stamp my foot. "I'm so angry I could eat peas."

"Yeah, I don't think that's the saying—"

"Am I invisible?" I ask, unable to stop myself.

She blinks rapidly like she's having a hard time keeping up. "Invisible?"

"That's why I'm angry. Because a lot of the time, it's like I'm there until it's inconvenient and then, poof! I'm gone. They just forget I exist. This happens to me over and over again."

Daisy side-eyes me as she whacks the brush across her palm a few times. "Who are you asking?"

"What do you mean?"

"I mean," she begins as she straightens up her supplies, dropping brushes in jars and closing tubes of paint. "Are you asking best friend, tough critic Daisy? Or sweet, kooky Daisy?"

"Um..." I hesitate, wondering if it bothers Daisy that we all think she's a bit eccentric.

She carries jars to the slop sink. As she fills them with water, she shouts over her shoulder, "Like, your zany, circle-casting friend might say, 'Are you kidding me? You're the opposite of invisible! You're neon! The life of the party! Everyone loves you.'"

"Which is part of the truth. But best friend Daisy would tell you the rest of it." Turning off the water, she holds up a hand. "And don't worry, I know, I know, I'm not your best friend. Leia is."

Not knowing what else to say, I argue, "I can have more than one best friend."

She shakes her head definitively. "I don't think so. The word best means there's someone at the top of the list."

"It's just that I've known Leia since we were toddlers."

"And I'm not a real Climaxian because I moved here in middle school. And then"—she gasps theatrically—"I left for college and didn't come right back."

"Well, I left for college and didn't come right back."

Daisy holds up her hands like, *I'm just callin' it like I see it.*

Needing to make her feel better, I add, "Anyway, you were in the witchy crowd in high school, so we didn't really hang out."

"*Wiccans*, not witches."

She waves both hands in the air between us like she's scrubbing it. "You know what? Doesn't matter. Even if I'm only your second or third best friend, I'll tell you what I really think. If you want me to."

I'm not sure if I do or I don't but I say, "I want to know."

"Okay, then." She clears her throat and then pins me with the gaze she uses when students say they don't like an assignment. It's a little scary. "People don't usually notice the doormat unless there's mud on their shoes. Then they just look long enough to make sure they've scraped it off before continuing on their merry way."

I take a step back from her. "Are you saying I'm a doormat?"

"I'm not saying you *are* a doormat, I'm saying you *act* like one."

"I don't think I get the difference," I say, still smarting at the insult even though I asked for it.

"Who ignored you this time?" Before I can answer, she

nods like she read it on my face. "It's Josh. What did he do?"

Too exhausted to resist but too embarrassed to share all the details, I just give her the basics. "Things got romantic over the weekend, but when we got back and the ship hit the fan, he said it had all been a mistake." I explain how Mabel was lost, then add, "Even after I found her, he couldn't, or wouldn't, look at me."

She sits with this for a long moment before saying, "That must've been pretty scary for him."

"Since I can't have kids, I wouldn't know," I snap.

She nods like, *Aha!* "So that's what this is about?"

"What do you mean?"

"You thinking you're not good enough for him because you can't make babies?"

"Of course not. It's about him giving up on us at the first bump in the road. And acting like I no longer exist."

"If that's what you say," she says, obviously not buying it.

"You don't think that's it?"

She starts pushing chairs under tables. "There are two sides to every story."

"I guess. Maybe."

"New relationships are fragile things." She stops straightening the room to point at me. "Especially new relationships forged away from home, away from work—"

"We did get some work done! I learned a ton and networked and am really inspired."

"Fine." She flicks a hand in the air as she begins to fold up easels. "Away from routine. Away from everyday responsibilities."

I have to stifle a sigh because she's probably right.

"You know I'm right."

"So what do I do?"

She winces.

"What? I don't have to grovel, do I? I didn't do anything wrong. Did I?"

She presses her lips together, like she's in pain.

"What!?"

"You're not gonna like it."

"Just spit it out."

"I'm back to the doormat thing."

"Oh." My belly twists with that yucky feeling when you're suddenly ravenous and nauseous at the same time.

She stalks over to me to place a hand on each of my upper arms, her grip almost painful. "You do need to give Josh a chance to tell his side of the story. But first, you're going to have to speak up for yourself in the other areas of your life. With your family"—she waves a hand around the room—"and here at the center."

"At CPR? I don't have a problem here."

Daisy lets out a long-suffering sigh. "Avery. You do the work of three people, you teach a class that isn't in your job description, and you volunteer for every other little extra thing." She gives me a little shake. "Boun-dah-ries. You need to set them."

"What does this have to do with Josh?"

She pulls out two chairs from under the worktable and sits down, indicating that I should too. A little unnerved, I sit.

"Speaking from experience," she begins, "you'll never be able to see and hear what Josh is really saying, how he really feels about you, if your own assumptions are shouting too loud inside your noggin."

"But what does that have to do—"

She holds up a hand. "You came in here assuming that the people closest to you don't see you or hear you. Right?"

"Okay, but I was angry."

"So turn that anger into action. Make a change. Convince yourself that you are worthy of being seen and heard."

"How do I do that?"

"By asking for what you want."

"But what if they say no?"

"When you ask, you have to tell them why you're asking. The reasons why the status quo isn't working for you. Don't let them off the hook."

"What if they still say no?"

"Then you have to decide if you're willing to live or work with people who don't respect you. But, honestly, Avery? I don't think that's going to happen."

When Jared drove me to CPR, all I could think about was getting home and crawling into bed, hiding under the covers, and crying myself to sleep. But after talking to Daisy, I'm thrumming with energy.

Because I suspect she's right.

Even though it feels selfish, I need to take my own advice. I may not be a parent, but I am a caregiver, and I have to figure out how to take care of myself, or I'll end up bitter and alone and mad at the world.

Not even sure what I'm going to say or do when I get home, I'm a little disappointed that Carla and her wife Sarah have left already because I'd been thinking that they'd be easier to confront. They're the ones who have barely helped out with Mom and Dad. Instead, when I walk into the kitchen, my mom offers to heat up some lasagna for me.

"Sarah made it. It's somehow good for you and tastes good."

"Um, sure. Thanks."

My mom bustles around for a few minutes, plating leftovers and starting the microwave, before pouring me a glass of fizzy water. She's been on an upswing for the past week or so, which is great, but there's a part of me that hopes she wasn't like this all weekend. Not that I want her to suffer, but it doesn't help my cause if Carla didn't see what it's really like here most of the time.

After she sets the food in front of me, she asks, "How was your conference?"

Jeepers. I almost forgot about the conference. "Good. I learned a lot."

I push the pasta around to let the steam out. And to will myself to eat it.

"What's wrong, honey?"

"Nothing. Just tired." I shake my head, knowing I should talk to my mom about needing my own life, my own space, but not sure how to start. "Did you have a good weekend?"

My mom doesn't like to talk about her health. I can hardly blame her. It must be so hard to never know how you're going to feel when you wake up. Not to mention how frustrating it is that doctors still don't know how to treat chronic COVID.

"It wasn't bad. We didn't do too much. Sarah spoiled us with her cooking."

My sister's wife is an excellent chef. Usually, I'd be scarfing down anything she made. Tonight, though, I'm too full of feelings to fit anything else inside.

"I heard about Mabel Harmon going missing. And that you helped find her."

"It was no big deal. Josh—um, they—the Harmons were very worried, of course. But it was pretty easy for me to find her."

My mom blows out a breath. Even without looking at her I can tell it's an irritated one. "Avery Catherine Mills. I wish you'd tell me what's wrong."

"Nothing's wro—" A sob fills my throat, cutting off my words and making me a liar.

She rubs a hand up and down my back. "Whatever it is, it'll be okay."

"I don't think that's possible."

"Just get it off your chest. You'll feel better."

"Fine," I say, turning to face her. There's no way I'm getting into what is or isn't happening with Josh and me, but there is one thing I can't put off any longer. "It's Playgroup. Only three families are signed up for the next session. With the restructuring that's happening, it's probably going to get cut."

My mom doesn't say anything, and I suddenly feel terrible. "I'm sorry, Mama. I did everything I could to save it."

She squeezes my arm. "I'm not upset, sweetheart."

"You're not?"

"I knew it wouldn't last forever. It's obvious that people need different things these days. Your siblings wouldn't be able to take part in a program like Playgroup, since everyone works."

My siblings who, unlike me, are capable of producing grandchildren. Shoving that bitterness aside, I face my mom again. "I really hoped, with more people working remotely, that we'd get more interest."

She pats my shoulder. "People are busy. Hopefully, they're finding community in other ways."

Feeling slightly better, I manage to eat about half of the lasagna before telling my mom that I need to get to bed. We work together tidying up the kitchen, and then she gives me a hug. "I love you, Avery."

"Love you too, Mama."

Just lugging my suitcase up the two flights to my room is exhausting but I make myself unpack, knowing I'll appreciate it in the morning. But when I realize that I must've left one of my favorite Vans at the retreat center, I just crumple onto the bed and hug the remaining lime green sneaker to my chest, letting out the few tears left in my ducts. Crying gets me all sweaty and as I'm wrestling out of my clothes, my hand pokes through a hole in the sleeve of my fleece. Staring at it, I realize I must've ripped it either climbing up or down the tree. At least Mabel's home, I remind myself, safe and warm in her room instead of alone, frightened, and cold in the woods.

When I dig my phone out of my bag to put it on the charger, there are texts and missed calls from Josh, but I can't face him right now. Anyway, I got the message. The weekend was a mistake. What else is there to say?

There're also a few messages from my siblings.

CARLA

Back in Syracuse.

And I'm exhausted.

My heart pounding, Daisy's words echoing in my ears, I begin to type.

I hold my breath as dots appear and disappear from my sister and brother for a few moments. Then they disappear altogether. Just as I'm about to start typing something like, *Forget about it, it's okay, I'll figure it out,* the phone rings, my sister's face flashing on the screen.

"Hello?"

"Hey," Carla says. "Brad's on too."

"Hey, Aves," my brother says.

They don't say anything else, so I ask, "What's up?"

"It's late and we all have work tomorrow so I'm just going to say it. I think Mom and Dad should move to a retirement place."

My brain freezes up because her words are not at all what I was expecting to hear. I hadn't really thought about what we should do, I suppose. Just that I can't do this anymore.

"You there?" Carla asks.

"Yeah, I just... but they're not that old."

"Not like a nursing home," Carla says. "More like a community. They'd have their own house but it'd be smaller. And they'd have easy access to activities and maybe even doctor's offices."

"Can they afford something like that?"

"Carla called me over the weekend, and I've done some research," Brad says. "There are a couple places just over the county line. They'd have to sell the house, of course."

"I felt it out with Mom and Dad. They're open to the idea," Carla says.

"Why didn't you tell me about this?"

"We just didn't want you to think we were kicking you out," Carla says. "Because, well, you'd have to move."

"I'm only here because of Mom and Dad," I say, hating that I sound like the bratty little girl they always complained about, but unable to be anything but defensive.

"Well, you did move in after everything went down in Atlanta," Carla says. "And then you just stayed, so..."

Remembering my talk with Daisy, I sit up straight and speak slowly. "I stayed because they needed someone."

"Does that mean you'd have somewhere to go if we sell?" Brad asks.

"I'd have to find a place." My heart thumping with fear, worried that my brother and sister will think I'm complaining for no reason, I make myself add, "And prices have gone up. A lot."

"I noticed," Brad says. "That's why Mom and Dad can afford to move. They'll get a decent price for the house. Things are cheaper outside of town."

I could move to the county too, I suppose. But I like

being close to work. To my friends. And if I'm not going to be a doormat anymore, I need to stand up for myself.

"I'd like to be recompensed for the time I've spent taking care of our parents." My voice is wobblier than I'd like, but I press on. "I haven't minded doing it, of course, but it has, um, limited my career choices."

After a beat that seems to last forever, my brother and sister talk at the same time.

"Oh, okay."

"We could do that."

"Like, what are you thinking?" Brad adds.

"I don't know. Enough to help me with a downpayment on my own place."

Brad and Carol bat around some ideas for a few moments before Brad sums it up by saying, "This is totally doable, Aves. I'm sorry we didn't think of it before."

"The family has saved a lot by having you there for the past couple years," Carol says. "We would've been paying a fortune in home healthcare. Plus, Mom said there's no way Dad would be as good about doing his PT without you badgering him. They appreciate what you've done too, honey."

Brad promises to run some numbers and talk Mom and Dad through the possibilities and a timeline. After we all sign off, I sink into my pillows, equally wired and exhausted. It took a lot to ask for what I deserve, but I was rewarded for doing it. Things won't always go my way so easily, but I guess it's true that it doesn't hurt to ask.

In fact, in this situation, it would've been hurtful not to ask. My parents might've avoided doing what's best for them because they wouldn't want to leave me in the lurch.

It's too late to make a difference between Josh and me,

and with the promise of a bit of financial freedom, I realize that I could leave Climax altogether if I wanted.

But it's not just Josh keeping me here. I love my hometown. I love my friends. And I even love my job, even though it's not what I set out to do. It might be torture to have to work with Josh without being a part of his life, but I can rise above it because I want to make CPR a place that serves our community.

I'm committing to Climax.

chapter
twenty-four

AVERY

I take a deep breath and count to ten but I still want to throw my laptop across the room. Not because I'm mad at Josh. I just don't want anybody to make decisions about CPR kids' programming until I've had my say.

I always thought that what Daisy called being a doormat was just being kind and generous with my time. But over the past few days, I've realized that a little gremlin of resentment hides underneath that helpful facade. When I'm assertive instead of passive, I can be the one to make things happen.

Best of all, I kind of like this version of myself.

It's a lot easier to be productive when you're not running around taking care of everyone but yourself. And learning how to say no, even to just a few things, has opened up all kinds of mental space to focus on things that are important to me.

I finally got Leia to share the complete survey results with me, and after reading through them, it's crystal clear that Playgroup has to go. The highest priority for families

233

now is after-school care, preferably a program that includes enrichment. It's hard for working parents—even ones working from home—to pick their kids up and drive from one activity to another. Even harder to cough up the money to pay for things like art classes or language lessons. But colleges expect applicants to have those things on their resumes.

Meanwhile, they're getting cut from school budgets right and left.

If CPR could provide these activities in one place after school, it would go a long way toward fulfilling that need. But we have the same problems parents do: costs and transportation. I know there's an answer. I can feel it tickling the back of my skull. But it just won't reveal itself.

"Sweet baby Cheez-Its!" I yell in an effort to jog something—anything—loose from my brain.

"You know kids don't believe in your so-called swear words, Aunt Avery." Riley Blake intones this from my doorway with the practiced ennui of a fourteen-year-old going on forty. She and her twin brother Owen aren't related to me, but I love being their honorary aunt.

"Says you," I shoot back. "Total bullnickles anyway, because you did."

Leia's daughter rolls her eyes in the exact same way her mother did when we were in middle school. "When I was *five* maybe."

"Exactly. My target audience."

She leans against the doorframe. "What's making you so *dadgum* upset anyway?"

"You know I stopped using that one. Kids kept begging me for dad gum."

"Whatev, Aunt Avery."

I'm about to shoo her out so I can concentrate, when I realize that she's exactly what I need. One of the walls I keep running into in my research is regarding teen jobs in Greene County. Either there are no jobs for young people during the school year, or the jobs that exist aren't advertised. Maybe the actual teens can fill me in on their employment situation. "You know, you just might be able to help me with this. Is your brother around?"

Instead of pulling out her phone to text him, Riley just turns her head and yells, "Ohh-wen! Get your bench in here!"

I look down so Riley doesn't see my smile. She probably doesn't even realize she's substituted "bench" for "butt."

Owen appears, panting, a few moments later. "Sup."

"Aunt Avery needs us, Shorty."

"Stop calling me that."

When he attempts to shove her, she deftly ducks under his arm and glides into the room. "Just callin' it like I see it."

Owen follows her, chest out. "You're like, half an inch taller than me."

"Like two inches you mean. I thought you were the math wiz."

"I am. And you need glasses." He straightens. "Right, Aunt Avery?"

I hold up my hands. "Not getting involved. But I do have a favor to ask."

"What do we get for it?" Owen asks.

Riley hip checks him before flopping into a chair. "Shut up, Shorty. You don't get paid for a favor."

"Not even candy?" he asks hopefully before sitting down next to her.

"Don't tell your dad." I pull a box out of my bottom drawer and we each take a piece of locally made fudge.

"So what's the fav?" Riley asks between licking her fingers. It's like she speaks in texts these days.

"Weelll," I begin, moving papers around until I find a legal pad. "I'm wondering if you two think there'd be a demand in your peer group for after school jobs?"

"Definitely," Owen says at the same time that Riley asks, "Like, what kind of jobs?"

"Working with elementary school kids."

Twin sets of eyes widen slightly, then twin heads whip to face each other. Some sort of twin mind meld happens for a few moments before they turn back to me.

Owen says, "Well, it depends."

"Yeah," Riley says. "We'd have to have a noncompete clause in our contract."

"A what now?"

Riley crosses her legs and leans back in her chair. "It's not easy working with teens' schedules."

Owen shrugs. "That's why we created the app."

"App? What app?"

Riley kicks her brother. "Owen."

"What? I thought we were—"

"Yeah, but not like every detai—"

"It's Aunt Avery." Owen points at me. "She's too old to figure shit like this out."

"Owen. Language," I say before adding with a shudder, "I'm too old? For what?"

After another silent exchange, Owen makes a *you do it* gesture at Riley. She sighs and sets her elbows on her knees. "Owen and me have a babysitting business. Parents and teens subscribe to our app, and we match them for gigs."

I knew my friends' kids were smart, but this is next level. "How long has this been going on?"

"Um..." Riley looks at Owen, like she can see the timeline in his face. "We started babysitting when we were twelve after taking that class your mom offered. Then we got so popular we started farming out the jobs to other people. Then Owen made the app a couple months ago."

"But your mom always says you're too busy to babysit."

"We're too busy running a business to babysit for free for her friends," Riley clarifies.

"Anyway," Owen adds. "Riley would rather manage people than actually babysit."

"Well, yeah, duh. Who wouldn't?"

"She likes bossing people around," he adds.

She huffs. "Also, so I can choose who I sit for, dummy."

"The people with the best snacks?" he asks.

"The people with the best rules. Whose kids have, like, bedtimes." She shrugs. "And snacks."

I sit back in my chair, mind reeling for a moment before circling back to my own problem. I've been hoping we could use teenagers to do the bulk of the work. It would give them something meaningful to do after school, and we'd only have to pay real salaries to a couple extra staff members to act as supervisors. "So... do you guys, like, have teen jobs covered already?"

Riley tips her head to the side, nodding slowly. "I think there's a market share for this. Especially on the parent side of things. Our prices are too high for a lot of families. Plus, it's harder for kids without cars. As it is, we have to match kids our age with families they can bike to."

"Or if it's the weekend, the parents drive," Owen adds.

"That's the other issue," I say. "I'm not sure what to do about transportation."

"What about school buses?" Owen asks.

"What about them?"

"A couple of the bus routes go right by CPR."

"They do?"

"How do you think we get here?" Riley asks.

I'd never thought about that. "So, both the students attending aftercare and the students working for us would just ride the bus?"

"I mean, you'd have to talk to whoever makes up the schedules and routes, but yeah," Riley says.

"Then they can all get picked up by their parents at dinnertime," Owen says.

I'm jotting down notes as fast as I can, getting really excited about this. Parents might want to take a fitness or art class at the end of the workday before picking up their kids. Or they could just chat outside, meeting their neighbors. CPR aftercare could be the kind of community builder Playgroup used to be.

"But do you think enough teens would be interested?" I ask, dreading their answer.

"Like we said, it's complicated," Riley says. "You'd have to work around sports practices."

"And other school activities."

"But those are all during school now."

"Not 4-H."

"True."

"But if it could be a thing to put on your, like, college resume—"

"People would totally be into that."

"Because except for farm harvests—"

"Or babysitting."

"There's, like, nowhere for kids our age to work."

"Only if their family has a business—"

"Like the diner, but—"

"Everyone who works there is a family member, and—"

As they go on like this, finishing each other's sentences, arguing about one point, agreeing on another, it suddenly hits me. They remind me of Leia and Eli back in high school. And that mouth twist Owen just did—that was Eli too.

Son of a *bitch*.

Riley gasps. "Aunt Avery! Did you just cuss for real?"

"Um, no." I jump up from my seat and move papers around. "I said son of a biscuit, like I always do, but that's bad enough. Thanks for the info, guys, but I just realized I'm supposed to..."

I have no idea what I'm supposed to do with this info. If it is actually information. If Leia wanted me to know that Travis isn't the twins' father, she would've told me. Maybe not back in high school, when the year and a half age difference made her seem much older, but surely she'd have confessed at some point in the past fourteen years.

I could be way off base, anyway. The two men have similar coloring. If Eli worked out, he'd have the same build as Travis. And even if it were true, Travis and Leia do an amazing job of co-parenting the twins; they always have. No need to stir up a hornets' nest for no good reason.

"Are you okay, Aunt Avery?"

"Of course. Thanks again for your help."

After a shared glance that makes it clear they know something's up, they say, "Ohhh-kaaay" in tandem before Riley pushes Owen out of the way so she can beat him out the door.

"Does this look like a penis?"

I never had a one-on-one meeting with the mayor of Climax before, but this is not how I imagined things would go. The woman looks more like a New York fashionista than a small-town bureaucrat, but that makes her query and the picture she's holding up even more confusing.

"Um, rocket ship is the first thing that came to mind, actually," I fib. Not saying the p-word to the mayor, even if she said it first.

"Ugh. This damn artist we hired to create a new logo for Climax keeps making the clock tower look like a pecker."

"Maybe if they made those bushes less prominent," I suggest, pointing at the rounded forms at the base of the tower.

"Those don't even exist in real life! I told her I need more City of Love, less City of Dying by Mercury Poisoning, but I can't have a logo that looks like a schlong! And the neon glow? It's like we're selling radioactive sex toys or something."

Muttering obscenities that would make a sailor blush, she slaps the paper with the offending image face down on her desk before looking up at me like she forgot I was here. With a flick of her hand, she orders me to sit.

Flinching slightly, I perch on the edge of a chair. But before I can hand her a copy of my proposal, she folds her hands in front of her and leans closer. "Speaking of our clock and its magical properties, how was your"—she waggles her eyebrows suggestively—"weekend away with Climax's newest eligible bachelor?"

Since Eli was the one who was supposed to go to the conference, I ask, "You mean Elijah Ransom?"

She huffs. "No, not Ransom. He's obviously hung up on someone from his past. I mean the adorable, widowed father. Find any harmony with Mr. Harmon?"

"But Josh wasn't even supposed to go on the trip. Nor was I, for that matter. How do you—"

She waves an irritated hand in the air. "It's my job to know everything that goes on in this town, missy."

High school civics was a long time ago, but I'm pretty sure that gossiping about town employees' love lives is not in the mayor's job description.

"Especially when it means I might get a fresh story for the CCC." She picks up a copy of the town's weekly paper and opens it to point at a column on the second page. "The Climax Clock Column, see? I'm hoping to revive interest in our town as a romantic getaway with tales of the clock that predicts true love."

I clear my throat, needing to get back on track. "Mr. Harmon and I did indeed have a fruitful weekend—"

The mayor gasps, a hand to her heart.

"Not that kind of fruit," I assure her, even as my cheeks heat just saying his name. "I'm sorry to disappoint you, but I am here to talk about a proposal for a new after-school childcare program at CPR. Inspired by a workshop at the conference," I add, in response to her frown.

"Fine," she says on a sigh. "I guess that's important too."

Fifteen minutes later, I have the mayor's stamp of approval. Problem is, she pointed out that Trede will have to sign off on it, since it requires a shift in resources. I'm not ready to talk to Josh, so I suppose that means I'm going straight to the top.

I just hope Eli remembers who I am this time.

chapter
twenty-five

JOSH

Trusting myself isn't going so well so far. I stayed up late, supposedly catching up on work, but in actuality checking my phone every few minutes—only to discover each time that Avery wasn't replying to my messages. I can't stop going over every little moment from the week-end, either. From Avery laughing hysterically while hanging upside down on the ropes course to the way she chanted my name when she came all over my face.

The only thing I can't remember is what happened after I heard my mom say Mabel was missing. Everything from those words to the moment I held my daughter in my arms again is a total blank.

After falling into bed sometime in the wee hours only to toss and turn, I must've fallen asleep at some point because I wake up to screams from Mabel. When I burst into her room, I'm both relieved and worried to see her having a meltdown over what to wear to school. Somehow, my mom gets Mabel and me out the door, but we're late enough to school that I have to endure the flirty chat from the school secretary while she writes Mabel a late slip. Then talk my child down from her worry that she'll get in trouble.

When I finally make it to work, I spend the day catching up on emails and calls, attend three useless meetings, and stare at my computer, trying to figure out what I'm supposed to be doing. In between checking my phone for messages from Avery.

On the drive home, I fantasize about sneaking up to my room and passing out instead of showing up for my family but when I pull up in front of the house to find my in-laws' car in the driveway, it truly takes everything I've got to get out of the car.

If I run away, they can't take my kids from me.

Wrong, Josh. That just gives them more proof that you can't do this on your own.

But when I walk inside, instead of finding scowling faces sitting stiffly around the living room—what usually happens when the Kingstons visit—my in-laws are on the floor actually playing with my children.

I should be happy to see it, but instead I'm stuck in a mix of feelings. Sad that Lisa never saw this. Angry that they never acted like this before. Worried that this is just a tactic to get the kids to like them so when they swoop in with their expensive New York lawyers to take them away, the kids won't freak out.

And what do I know? Maybe the kids would be better off with them. Instead of a father who can't seem to get anything right, they'd have nannies to take care of their every need, the best schools, all the opportunities wealth affords.

But then I remember: that's how Lisa was raised. And she wasn't happy.

I have an urge to barge into the room and demand to know what's going on, but instead, I take a deep breath and count to five before saying, "Daddy's home!"

Usually when Jack and Tilly Kingston want to talk to me, they summon me to the family's corporate offices in midtown Manhattan on the top floor of a property I think they've owned since the beginning of time, or at least since New York was still a colony ruled by a king.

Until this week, they've never visited Climax.

They've never sat down to dinner with Mabel and Percy. Or supervised bathtime or read them stories. But they do all these things today. They're not quite sure what to make of Percy's need to run naked up and down the hall after his bath, but to be honest, this habit might be mystifying to anyone. I'm sure I look like a madman as I pretend to chase him, growling like an ogre, but my son's shrieks of laughter when I catch him push those thoughts to the side. He loves our little ritual, and he loves when we snuggle in bed afterward while he tells me stories about his stuffies that make no sense until he falls asleep.

I don't know what they're here for, so I gird myself for the worst when I head back downstairs to face the music. I find them in the living room, laughing about something with my parents. When I enter, the laughter fades, and my dad stands. "I need to, uh, check some emails."

Tilly clears her throat. "I apologize for keeping you up. We truly appreciate your hospitality."

"We just wanted to discuss a few things with Josh," Jack says. When my mom stands too, he holds out a hand. "You're welcome to stay and hear what we have to say."

My mom catches my eye, a question in hers, and I give her a quick nod. *I can handle this.* "I've got to check on a couple things too. But it was lovely to see you. Please come back anytime."

The moment my parents leave the room, the Kingstons turn as one to face me, and I hold up a hand. "Look, I know I screwed up. Losing Mabel is the worst thing that's ever happened to me."

Realizing what I just said, I add, "Except for losing Lisa, of course."

Jack clasps Tilly's hand. "That's why we're here."

My heart drops to my gut and then ricochets back up to my skull to pound in my ears so loud that I can't hear what he says next. When they continue to stare at me expectantly, I make myself ask, "I'm sorry, what did you say?"

"We want to apologize," Tilly says. "We can't tell Lisa how sorry we are for not being the parents she needed us to be. But we don't want to make that mistake again with her children."

Blinking, I try to make sense of what she's saying as I sink onto the couch across from them. "Okay?"

Tilly looks at Jack like she's asking for permission, and when he nods, she turns back to me. "Jack had a bit of a health scare last month."

"I'm sorry to hear that," I say automatically.

He nods. "I'll be fine. It was a cardiac event and I'm making some lifestyle changes."

"And taking his medication," Tilly says, her expression equal parts affection and reprimand.

"The reason we're telling you this, is that the experience, on top of Lisa's passing, led us to some..."

Jack looks to Tilly, who picks up his sentence. "Soul-searching. About our priorities. And after some counseling, we've realized that we need to make some changes."

"Top of the list is prioritizing our relationships with our grandchildren. The only connections we have to our daughter."

"I found her journals when we cleaned out her old room in our apartment. Reading them—" Tilly breaks off, obviously overcome with emotion.

Jack pats her hand. "She was suffering, and we never knew."

Feeling like I'm about to jump off a building, I make myself say what I need to. "I'm so sorry to hear all this. The health issue, and what sounds like losing Lisa all over again. But you can't take my children. They're finally getting settled here. I know you can give them more than I can but I'm their father."

Tilly's brows come all the way together. "Take them? Is that why you think we're here?"

"Well, yeah. Last time I was in New York, your lawyers said—"

Jack waves a hand in the air. "I fired that firm. I apologize if they said anything that had you concerned. They were not acting with our priorities in mind."

"It's obvious you and your parents are doing a wonderful job raising them," Tilly adds. "And that you took care of Lisa the best you could."

"So, what is it you want?" I ask, truly confused.

"Just to know our grandchildren, dear." Tilly looks down at her hands clasped in her lap. "We just hope it's not too late."

"I, uh, well..." I'm struggling for words. This conversation is so unlike any I've had with Lisa's parents before, it takes several beats before I can settle on what to say. "That sounds like a great idea, and I'm happy to help make it happen."

Tilly's parents look so relieved I almost burst out laughing, because it's exactly what I'm feeling. Here I was worried that they hated me, that they thought I wasn't good enough for their daughter, but the real situation is the exact opposite of what I'd assumed.

Which makes me wonder: are my assumptions about what Avery's thinking and feeling wrong too? And if so, what is the truth? Does she hate me for pushing her away when I panicked? Or was the weekend away just a fling for her? If it's the latter, my perceptions are totally out of whack. She said she wanted to take things public, didn't she? Or was she just humoring me?

And how do I learn the truth if she won't speak to me?

A few days later, I still haven't heard from Avery, but I do wake up at dawn with an idea. On its surface, it doesn't really seem to have anything to do with Avery or our relationship or apologizing, but I have a sense that if I can make it happen, it'll help convince her to give me a second chance.

Maybe this is what my mom meant when she told me to trust myself?

But when I get to Trede, proposal for my new idea in hand, Eli's not in his office. I ask his assistant to let him know that I'd like to meet with him and then head to my own office, where I find Eli scowling at me. "I thought I was supposed to stay out of things at the rec center."

"How did you get here before me?"

He looks at his watch. "Looks like you're late."

"But I was just in your office. Asking to meet with you."

"Guess I beat you to it," he says. "Now, can you answer my question?"

He didn't really ask a question, but I don't want to make him mad when I need to get him on my side, so I say, "I have an idea that will make Leia Blake happy."

"Is it the aftercare program? Because I already know about that."

"Aftercare?"

"Did you not just spend the weekend at a conference with that blond woman from CPR? What's her name? Starts with an *A*?"

Not sure where this is going, hoping I'm not in trouble for either sleeping with her or making her mad, I say, "Avery Mills and I did attend the conference, but we split up to cover as many sessions as possible."

"And now you've split up with her romantically too?"

Eli's in my desk chair. I seem to have lost all control of this conversation, so I give up, dropping in the guest chair. "I'm confused."

"Imagine how I feel. You're the one who's supposed to be in charge of community relations, but yesterday both this Avery woman and the mayor hunted me down. Avery has this after-school program idea where kids get bussed to the rec center and the big ones get paid to babysit the little ones. The mayor is in favor of that, but she's upset because you and Avery broke up."

He points a finger at me. "She said I have to get you two back together because, and I quote, 'I can't have a clock that misfires.' Now who has a reason to be confused?"

Since I've obviously failed, yet again, I stand to take my punishment. "I'm doing the best I can here, Eli. If that's not good enough, then maybe you should put us both out of our misery and fire me."

"What? Is that what you want?"

"No, of course not. I'm just... I feel like I'm doing a bad job. Here, at home... everywhere."

"Well, I'm not going to fire you because you've had an off week. This isn't Wall Street."

While I'm ripping off Band-aids, I decide to go for them all. "Did you give me the job in the first place because of Lisa?"

To his credit, he doesn't seem thrown by the topic change. "If I'm being honest, yeah. I felt guilty because I wasn't a good friend to her when she needed me."

"So you knew she was unhappy?"

He nods and lets out a heavy sigh. "But I didn't know how to help."

"Welcome to the club."

"But that's not why I want you to stay. You're good with people, at least when you don't have your head up your ass. And I like having you around."

I believe him. And I think he's right. I am good with people. My mom is right too. I can trust that I know what to do. I'm going to fuck up on occasion, my kids will probably still need therapy, but I'm not quitting any of it.

"Okay then. Tell me why you moved Trede to Climax."

"This is connected how?"

"Just trust me, it is."

He hesitates a beat before spitting out, "I moved here for a year and a half in high school and it's the only place I've ever really been happy."

"How did your parents end up in Climax?" I seem to remember them being diplomats or something.

"They didn't. When my parents were stationed in Suriname, I got kicked out of boarding school, so they sent me to live in Climax with my aunt Greta. My mother's sister. She was an artist and was one of the founding members of the co-op in the old foundry." Eli gets up and moves to the window. "You can just see it from here."

I get up to stand next to him and he points at a building near the clock tower.

"It's the one that's made of stone instead of brick." Shoving his hands in his pockets, he walks back into the room. "Anyway, she had a boyfriend who was a carpenter, and they worked on her house together. I learned a lot from both of them. About all kinds of stuff. And I was happy. But my parents didn't think I'd get into a good school if I stayed for senior year, so they shipped me off to a prep school."

"Did you ever visit after that?"

"I didn't. But I kept in touch with my aunt. We wrote letters. And when she passed away, she left me her house." He frowns, staring off into the middle distance. "I was planning to sell it but when I came back to see it one more time, I couldn't. I took a walk up the river, saw the brick-works, and decided to move everything here."

"So, not for business reasons? Not because property taxes were low or you scored incentives from the state?"

"Well, those things were true too." He narrows his eyes at me. "Are you going to tell me why you needed to know this?"

"There was a session at the conference on the issue of workforce housing." Grabbing my briefcase, I pull out my proposal. "I want to turn the abandoned mall into a complex that provides homes that teachers, firefighters, and small business owners can afford." Handing him the printout, I add, "This is just an outline."

Eli looks it over briefly before handing it back to me. "This is really outside of our scope. Trede can't take on this big of a development project."

I cross behind my desk, refusing to take the papers. "It would serve your interests."

"How?"

"It would make Leia happy."

He frowns again but says, "Go on."

Summarizing what Avery told me a few weeks ago, leaving out a few details about Leia's relationship with Travis, I explain how Trede's relocation has exacerbated spiking home prices in Climax.

Eli shrugs. "I'll just buy her a house."

"I don't think that's really the point. Yes, Leia is worried that she's getting priced out, but she's also concerned about her friends and employees. Buying her a house doesn't help—wait a minute." My heart skips a beat. "That-that's it."

I'm on my feet and halfway out the door by the time Eli calls, "What's it?"

"Sorry, I just figured something out. I'll put together something more detailed, get some quotes, and circle back... um, later."

"You'd better fix things with that Avery person," he yells as I exit my office. "I need to stay on the mayor's good side."

"That's exactly what I'm going to do," I call over my shoulder as I sprint to the elevators.

chapter
twenty-six

AVERY

Bert Harmon has accompanied Percy to Playgroup for the past two weeks. Two days after we returned from the conference, he showed up, mumbling something about Frieda needing to stay off her ankle and Josh being swamped at work, but the real reason is obvious to me. Neither of them wants to see me again. Which hurts, especially because I felt such a close bond with Mabel, and I fall further in love with Percy every time I see him.

It makes the end of Playgroup both easier and harder to face.

For better or worse, I'm truly swamped at work. The mayor and the school superintendent are both so excited about the aftercare idea that they want to push it through for the spring semester. Leia used the opportunity to get the funding approved for another program admin which has freed up some of my time, but I'm still spending every free moment setting up systems so families can sign up, interviewing part-time hires to supervise the teen workers and lead enrichment activities, working with the school transpo people to reroute buses and drivers, marketing the program, and fielding a bazillion questions.

It's not easy, but it's fulfilling.

As well as a good funnel for the anger-fueled energy buzzing through me. I'm not letting the shirt-for-brains doctor or that son of a biscuit Peter make me feel like shiitake mushrooms anymore. Instead, at Daisy's suggestion, I've started a gratitude journal.

This morning, for instance, I'm grateful for the chance to live on my own for the first time in my life. My brother has secured a spot for my parents at a retirement community with on-site medical services as well as lots of social opportunities and a bus that drives them to both. A realtor friend of my sister's is eager to put the house on the market and my siblings have deposited a chunk of money in my savings account that just might be enough for a deposit on a small house in Climax.

The realtor also got me preapproved for a loan, so I've been trolling the real estate websites, ready to pounce on anything that seems doable, and secretly hoping my grandparents' old place will go up for sale.

Pressing send on the email that ticks off the final item of the morning's to-do list, I click over to check on listings before I take my lunch break.

And my stomach drops. "What in the halibut?"

"You okay?" Carl Conrad asks from the doorway to my office. "You look like someone died."

I just stare at the screen, trying to understand what I'm seeing.

He steps farther into the room. "Seriously, Avery. Should I call someone?" When I look up, he blanches. "Oh, no. Don't cry."

I swipe a hand across my face. "I'm not crying."

"Okay, well. Just in case." A blindingly white, pressed handkerchief appears in front of my face. "Take this."

I take it but return my attention to the screen. "How...?"

"Are you sure you don't, like, need anything?" Conrad asks, sounding like he really hopes I don't.

"What I need is for this forking house to not be sold after being on the market for, like, ten minutes." I'm so angry, the words feel like daggers coming out of my mouth, but it doesn't stop me from shooting laser eyes at Conrad. Just because he's standing there, not because I think our facilities manager can fix this problem. "Can you do something about that?"

"Um. Well, maybe."

Shocked at his answer, I just blink at him. "Really?"

"Lemme see the listing."

I turn my laptop around and he stoops to look at it, his large hands looking too big for the mousepad as he scrolls. "Hmm. Old house. That's good."

"Why?"

"How much you want this place?"

"More than anything."

He nods. "Gimme ten minutes."

I'm not sure if he really takes ten minutes, but when I look up from the computer again, he hands me a sealed envelope, saying, "It's in escrow, so the buyer can still back out. The inspector is at the house this afternoon, so high-tail it over there and give this to him. He'll know what to do."

"What will he do?"

"Find a reason why the buyer should back out. Roots

eating away the sewer main or mold in the walls." Conrad points at me, his expression serious. "We don't like to use this option unless it's an emergency but... gotta keep the sharks away from our homes somehow."

My curiosity is piqued, but I want my house more than I want intel, so I jump to my feet, grab my purse, and throw my arms around him. Or most of the way around, since I can't quite reach. "Thank you, Connie!"

He pats me awkwardly on the back. "All right, then. Go get your house."

chapter
twenty-seven

JOSH

Buying a little bungalow in Climax is somehow much more nerve-wracking than buying a condo in Manhattan. Probably because Kingston family accountants and lawyers took care of all the details when Lisa and I purchased our place in the city, just like they took care of selling it. Turns out, I've never done this before.

But here I am, offer accepted, waiting for the inspector to show up. Fiddling with the list of questions that I printed out from some online research, the package for Avery under my arm, I pace back and forth in an attempt to quell my nerves.

Hoping that I'm doing the right thing.

Just when I'm about to lose my nerve and call the realtor to say, I'm not sure what, something like, *You know what? Forget it, this was a mistake, who cares about the deposit,* a weathered work truck pulls up in front of the house. An equally weathered man climbs out of it to give me a nod and a terse, "You the buyer?"

I wave. "That's me."

"You got the code to get in?"

Remembering the email the realtor sent, I nod as I unlock my phone. "It's right here."

"Open 'er up and I'll be with you in a minute."

I punch in the code to get the door unlocked as he pulls some tools out of his truck, but as he walks up the front steps, a familiar-looking Subaru pulls up behind his truck. There are a lot of Subarus in this town, but I only know of one with a pink rubber duck on the tip of its radio antenna.

"Um," I say quietly to the inspector. "I need to hide from the woman who just pulled up in front of the house."

I slip inside and crouch behind the door just as her car door slams. Moments later, Avery greets the man and asks if the buyer is present.

"Yep. He's hiding right behind this door."

"Dammit, man!" I shout-whisper as I swing the door open.

"Josh?" Avery's face goes from pale to ghostly. "What are you doing here?"

Before I can answer, her expression shifts from shock to flat-out anger. "Wait. You stole my house from me? First, you drop me like a hot potato, and then you buy my grandmother's house?"

"I'll just be in the attic," the inspector says, walking right between us as if this kind of thing happens all the time in his world.

"This was, uh, supposed to be a surprise." My arms flap uselessly at my sides, wanting to wrap her in a hug. "So, surprise! Heh-heh."

She is not amused. Hands on hips, she just looks me up and down like she's seeing me in a whole new light. An unflattering one. "What, you were going to show up at CPR and say, ha-ha, I bought your dream house?"

I wince. "Well, yeah. Without the mean ha-ha."

Her head shakes like she can't even with me right now, but when she gasps and I follow her gaze to the object on the floor, I'm the one who can't believe how badly this is all going.

Clutching the single green sneaker that I must've dropped when I hid behind the door, she stares at me like I am her worst nightmare. "Why would you do this to me?"

The hurt washing over her face is a knife to my heart, but I deserve it. Hands shaking with the need to hold her, I say, "I'm not quite sure how I fucked this up so royally Avery, but this was all supposed to be a good surprise. I bought it for you."

Her jaw drops but before she can reject the offer I barrel on. "I know it doesn't solve the greater housing problem. I'm working on that too, though. We're looking for a developer to partner with for a workforce housing proj"—I wave a hand in the air, stopping myself from getting too sidetracked—"but that doesn't matter. I mean, it matters, of course but…"

I blow out a breath. "I'm trying to say that this house came on the market, I had the cash because of the sale of the condo in Manhattan, and I didn't want someone else to get it."

She just shakes her head slowly. "So you stole my favorite shoe and you're moving into my dream house?"

I shake my head quickly. "No, no! You are. Whenever you're ready. You can pay rent if you want, or you can use the money you're saving to pay for a caregiver for your parents. That doesn't matter to me. That condo money doesn't feel like mine anyway. But if you move in, and you can forgive me, it'd be a place we can be together. Without having to leave town. And as for the shoe, I found it in my suitcase and I thought that it'd be a fun surprise for you to find it here."

Her brow furrowed, she narrows her eyes like she's having a difficult time following my logic. "What about the kids?"

"The three of us will continue to live at my parents' place. And we will visit. If you'll have us."

Her mouth drops, her head still shaking, but she doesn't say yes. Or no.

That knife twists in my heart again, reminding me there's more to say. "And I also hope you'll forgive me for being a jerk. I don't even remember what I said when we pulled up in front of my parents' house. I saw my in-laws and I just panicked. I was sure they'd use Mabel getting lost to say I was an unfit parent and whisk her and Percy back to the city."

"Oh, Josh."

Her shoulders slump, and when a hint of something like compassion blooms in her face, I'm able to take a full breath for the first time since that call came through from my mom weeks ago. "Whatever you heard me say, it wasn't about us. Or you. Or the amazing weekend we shared. I loved every minute of it and would do it again tomorrow."

I hold out my hands, hoping she might be able to find a way to forgive me. When she takes them, I step closer, bringing both of her hands to my heart. "You are precious to me. You've brought hope to my life when I never thought I'd feel that again. You make me a better dad, a better man. I don't want to live my life without you in it, so Avery, please forgive me."

Her eyes fill, and her smile is wobbly, but she nods. "Thank you for the apology. And I'm sorry too."

"You don't—" I begin, but she stops me with a sharp shake of her head.

"I should've talked to you. I shut down because of what happened back when I woke up after that surgery and found out what I'd lost. I didn't stand up for myself then." She shakes her head again, slowly this time. "And I did the same thing when you said our weekend away was a mistake. I shut down and I ran. But I want to work on that. I know I can trust you up here"—she frees a hand to point to her temple and then her heart and her gut—"but I have to work on it here and here."

"And do you love me here?" I ask, placing a hand over her heart. "Because I need you to know that I'm in love with you. All of you."

She covers my hand. "I do. I love you, Josh Harmon. With all my heart."

Stepping even closer, I brush my lips to hers before murmuring, "What about here? And here? Or here?" I continue to ask, as her moans and whimpers answer my mouth and hands' exploration of the face and body I've missed more than I'd ever imagined possible. Just when I'm wondering if there's anywhere private in this unfurnished, uncurtained house, the clearing of a throat has me crashing back to reality.

"So which kind of job am I doing here?" The dust- and

cobweb-covered inspector holds up an envelope. "Conrad's version or the real version?"

Avery disentangles herself just enough to turn around and face the man. "You can save Conrad's version for another time. We want the real story on this one."

epilogue

AVERY

Waking up with the sun, snuggled in bed in my dream house—the one I co-own with Josh after having talked him into selling me half—Josh's morning wood pressed against my ass... it's my favorite way to greet the day.

Oh, yes. I said ass. I use any and all the words now, when they're right and fitting.

And everything about my world is right and fitting these days. Thinking about the woman I was last summer, overworked and harried and running from one thing to another just to avoid thinking about how unhappy she was —turns out, therapy is great for discovering such hidden truths—I couldn't feel more grateful for where and who I am now.

My parents are thriving, getting care that allows them both to be more active and more social. When I see them now, it's to enjoy their company rather than worry about what I need to do for them. Even better, my mom is enrolled in a new trial for chronic COVID treatment, and my dad's actually meditating, which he says helps with his pain. Along with what he calls his "special gummies."

Therapy has also helped me figure out what kind of work I want to do. Turns out I was pretty close. I love serving my community by providing healthy, safe, and fun activities for the citizens of Climax, so after a few long talks with Leia, I'm now officially the director of all programming. The difference is, I have an assistant to keep up with paperwork and schedules. She loves spread-sheets which means I love her.

Moving into this house while Josh and the kids remained at his parents' has allowed me to live by myself for the very first time. It seems I made some choices in the past—like moving in with Peter—because I was afraid to be alone. Now, after a full day of peopling, I love to escape to a space I've made my own.

Since I'm no longer caring for my parents and working sixty-hour weeks, it's unbelievable how much time I have. Time to walk in the woods, take those Zumba classes, hang out with my friends, even learn to quilt with the sewing machine and supplies I found in my parents' attic when we cleaned out their house.

Best of all, I have three people in my life who make every day an adventure—one of them sleeping next to me, the other two tucked into guest beds down the hall.

When Josh shifts behind me, I press his palm to my breast and my bum into his erection. If he's awake, we might be able to get in a little morning nookie before—

"Ca' we have pa'cakes?" Percy yells from the bedroom doorway.

Ah, well. Sexy times can wait.

"Sure thing, buddy. Just give me a minute to wake up."

Josh groans into my upper back before pressing a kiss to my neck. When I turn to face him, he kisses a trail across my shoulder, up my neck, and ending at my lips. I part my lips, needing more of him.

"Later," Josh murmurs, breaking the kiss and nodding at the bathroom door. "I'll be back in a sec."

He gives me a kiss to seal the promise before rolling out of bed and into his robe. As the bathroom door closes behind him, both kids clamber up onto the bed.

"Look, Avery!" Mabel shouts. "I made you a card."

"A card? It's not even my birthday."

"Me too!" Percy smushes an envelope onto my chest.

"Aww, you guys are the best." Shifting so that I'm sitting up against the headboard, I ask, "Should I open them?"

"Yes!" they say in unison.

One child bouncing in anticipation on either side of me, I rip open both envelopes. Percy's card is a very colorful and completely undecipherable scribble. "Aw, I love it, Perce!"

Mabel's has a beautiful drawing on the front. Less colorful, but I know what it is instantly: the four of us in front of this house. "You even put Jenny Linsky on the porch!"

She reaches over to unfold the card. "Read what it says!"

As I do, the bathroom door opens and Josh gasps. "Guys! You were supposed to wait."

Crossing to the bedside, he adds, "I had a whole romantic dinner planned."

Mabel lifts her hands like, *Oh well.* "Now we can have a romantic breakfast!"

Percy pats my hand. "Mama, why kwy-een?"

"Happy tears, Percy. I promise." He's never called me that before, and a full-on sob bursts out of me as I look up from Mabel's card. The card that reads, in very impressive block letters, "Will you be my mommy?"

I give Percy a sloppy kiss and then turn to Mabel. "The answer is yes." Mabel is less comfortable with physical affection, so I ask her first. "Can I kiss you?"

"The answer is yes," she says primly, before launching herself at me for an even sloppier sloppy kiss, which she breaks almost immediately to stand on the bed. "Yay! I can be a flower girl!"

As she bounces, Josh gets on the bed and walks on his knees to my side. Pulling a little velvet box from his pajama pocket, he meets my eyes as he opens it. "Avery Mills, love of my life, will you be my wife?"

My eyes flit from the ring to the excited, hopeful faces surrounding me and my body wriggles with joy. "Yes," I say to Josh. "I would love to be your wife and a part of your family."

"*Our* family," he says firmly, before sliding the ring on my finger. His eyes shining, he whispers, "You've made me the happiest man in town."

Then he pulls me in for the sloppiest kiss of all.

"What are those bells, Daddy?" Mabel asks.

Josh breaks the kiss and pulls away just far enough to meet my gaze. "They mean we're in love honey. And that we're going to live happily ever after."

Want more of Avery and Josh? Subscribe at karengrey.com to access an exclusive bonus epilogue! My VIPs will also be the first to hear about the next book in the Welcome to Climax series.

If you can't wait and want to stay in upstate New York, head on down to Fork Lick for Sam and Diane's one-night-stand to rivals-to-lovers story, *For Fork's Sake,* available wherever books are sold.

In the meantime, if you enjoyed this book, I'd be ever so grateful if you'd leave a review on Bookbub, Goodreads, Storygraph or wherever you purchased it. Thank you for supporting indie authors like me!

acknowledgements

I've had a difficult time hanging onto hope in the past few months (end of 2024; beginning of 2025 if you're reading this in the future) but even as I struggled, romance novels were a haven for me.

It's easy to think that writing and reading romance has no deep meaning and doesn't make a difference to the world at large. But I think it's too easy to make that assumption. I'm not the first person to say that romance is essentially about hope. Putting your heart on the line and making the effort to heal old emotional wounds require both courage and hope. Going on the journey with characters taking those risks is an exercise in courage and hope for readers.

So, dear reader, I hope this story has been such a venture for you (even if I didn't take you on an escape back in time!)

This book was inspired in part by many happy memories from my family's time living in Los Angeles. The TV show *Parks & Recreation* was definitely an influence, but the real-life Palms Rec Center on Olympic Boulevard in West

<h1 style="text-align:center">Acknowledgements</h1>

LA contributed many details to the story. Its facilities may have been aging and its athletic field may have tipped at a thirty-degree angle (something that actually got fixed after we moved away) but it was a wonderful place for kids to learn soccer and t-ball and art. My youngest and I took part in a program very much like Playgroup and my eldest's games were called by a sports director who, like Travis, knew the name of every child on the field.

Like raising kids, writing a book takes a village and I'm very, very grateful for my little author village. I gain so much from all the members of the WRP discord and the RAM Romcom FB group, but this time around critique partners Lainey Davis, Michelle McCraw, and Carla Luna were an essential part of the birth of this book. The town of Climax wouldn't exist without my Farm 2 Forking partners: Liz Alden, Lainey Davis, Ember Leigh and Erin Mallon. Many thanks to sensitivity reader Dana Sachs, and to my niece Ezri White for input on the tech industry. Finally, a whole passel of readers volunteered to beta read this book and shared invaluable feedback. Thanks to: Adrienne Patenaude, Amy Reierson, Elizabeth Taylor, Kristi Reetz, Kristie Galindo, Laura Black, and Michelle Tindall.

Many thanks to Kimberly Dawn for editing services and Marten at Flower Prince designs for the fantastic cover art and design. I'm also in awe of the reviewer and influencer team at HCB who help me get books and audiobooks in readers hands and ears. Thanks to all of you for the many ways in which you share your love of books!

Finally, I'm very grateful for the person from whom I learn about love and relationships every single day. I couldn't do this without you.

also by karen grey

What I'm Looking For: *The course of true love never did run smooth*, but in this smart and sexy retro rom-com with a finance-nerd heroine and a drama-geek hero, returns on love can't be measured on the S&P 500.

Forget About Me: An underwear model, a best friend's little sister, and a dog who steals the show make for an unforgettable mix in this bittersweet romantic comedy.

You Spin Me: If two lonely people fall in love over late-night phone calls, will meeting face-to-face make them, or break them? In this heartfelt, slow-burn retro romcom, it may be the end of a decade, but it's the beginning of a love story.

Child of Mine: A single mom gets a job offer she can't refuse but has to work side-by-side with the one-night stand that doesn't know he's a father. Of her daughter.

You Get What You Give: When a fiery redhead and the guy she thought was a one night stand turn out to be rivals, his family feud causes shockwaves bigger than the surf stirred up by the latest hurricane.

Hold On To Me: In this slow-burn, boss-assistant, entertainment biz romance, a bad cop movie production chief takes on a sexy assistant who challenges her every assumption.

I Want It That Way: She's a driver to the stars who just wants to get her tubes tied. He's a former child actor who needs to get back behind the wheel. A fake relationship seems like the perfect solution.

When I Come Around: When two besties work together on a movie out of town, a secret friends-with-benefits deal seems like a good idea. Until their friends weigh in.

For Fork's Sake: Grumpy, nerdy soil scientist Sam finds passionate, idealist Diane interviewing his grandma for her YouTube channel. Feathers fly between these farm business rivals!

The Single Dad's Guide to Recreation: He's the new-in-town single dad tasked with cutting costs at Climax Parks & Rec. She's the program director with classes on the chopping block. It should be easier for them to keep their hands off each other.

about the author

KAREN GREY is a *USA Today* bestselling and award-winning author of vintage romantic comedies with smart heroines and hunky heroes. Drawing on a long career as a performer, her retro 80's and 90's romances are populated with characters working both on- and off-stage in theater, TV and film while her contemporaries are drawn (almost) completely from her imagination. When not reading or writing, she's lounging at the beach or hiking in the mountains or cuddling with her cat.

(Author photo: Celestial Studios)

For the latest news and bonus materials, join her free VIP club at: karengrey.com

facebook.com/karengreyauthor

instagram.com/karengreyauthor

goodreads.com/karen_grey

bookbub.com/profile/karen-grey

tiktok.com/@karengreyauthor